Mark Your Brand Here

T

ↄOWF

PALO DURO
SHOOTOUT

Other books by Kent Conwell:

PALO DURO
SHOOTOUT

•

Kent Conwell

AVALON BOOKS
NEW YORK

To my grandson, Keegan,
and to Amy and Jason, his parents,
whose lives will never be the same.

And to my wife, Gayle.

Chapter One

Uniforms soggy with sweat, six Union soldiers lay scattered among limestone boulders heated to a blistering hundred and thirty degrees by the scorching rays of the August sun.

From his position on top of the ridge, Lieutenant Zeke Tanner wiped the perspiration from his broad forehead and squinted at the trail below. He shifted his gaze southward, his cool gray eyes searching for the first indication of the Confederate patrol that should pass just below.

"Hot enough to loosen the bristles on a wild boar," he muttered, dragging his tongue over his dry lips, wishing he was back in La Junta, Colorado, sipping a cold beer, and not down in Central Texas in the middle of Johnny Reb country attempting to pull off a spectacular hijacking of Confederate gold.

And if such a task wasn't dangerous enough, his orders instructed them to then transport the gold back to La Junta, a perilous journey through the middle of Comancheria, over thirty-two thousand square miles controlled by Comanche, Apache, and Kiowa. While his superiors were well aware of the risk, they believed it to be worth the gamble. By denying the Confederacy the gold, the war might end that much sooner.

A hundred thousand in gold. A cryptic grin curled his dry lips. For what he had planned, Comancheria didn't worry him. Suddenly, he stiffened and frowned at a cloud of dust billowing in the distance. Too much dust for a small patrol of Graybacks, he told himself.

Just over the horizon, three wranglers pushed a herd of ornery, hard-headed beeves northwest along the trail to Fort Chadbourne. The trail cut through a woodland made up of several hundred square miles of sun-baked grass under the scanty shade cast by stunted oak and wiry mesquite.

Riding swing, Josh Miles removed his Stetson and wiped the sweat from his forehead. He ran his fingers through his sandy hair, allowing the air to cool his damp scalp. On the other side of the small herd riding the off-swing, Leeboy Strauss grinned and shook his head. He cupped his hand to his mouth and shouted over the backs of the shuffling cattle, "It's sure hot! You reckon the chickens are laying hardboiled eggs yet?"

Josh grinned lazily and nodded. He tugged his hat

back on his head. They couldn't reach the fort too soon for him. Pushing fifty head of stupid, unpredictable critters over a hundred and twenty miles of rugged hill country and then through a waterless, rock-strewn prairie dotted with shriveled trees had just about worn his patience thin as Bull Durham paper.

Leeboy called out again. "How much farther, you reckon?"

Josh held up five fingers.

At the point of the herd rode their boss, JS Tipton, owner of the JS Bar back near Mason. JS wheeled his bay about and waved his arm to the northeast, indicating a small patrol of Confederate cavalry squatting around a small fire in the thin shade cast by a motte of stunted oak. The lieutenant waved. JS shouted, "Keep the herd moving, boys! I'll find out what them soldier boys are up to!"

The soldiers watched curiously as the herd passed. JS palavered with them a few moments, nodded, and headed back to the herd. Josh waved to the small contingent of soldiers although they were too far away to discern their features. A few of the soldiers returned his greeting.

"Heading for Chadbourne. Whipping themselves up some dinner. They'll be in later," JS said as he pulled his bay up beside Josh's sorrel. He shook his head. "Don't appear the war's going too good. Them old boys is wearing nothing but rags. The lieutenant even had a red patch sewed to the elbow of his jacket." He paused, eyeing the dog-tired cattle shuffling wearily along the dusty trail, their heads drooping. He drawled, "All things considered, we done made good time."

Josh nodded. "Reckon so. Be glad when it's all over."

The older man stroked his handlebar mustache, once black as the inside of a cow, now white as a Christian woman's petticoat. "We'll hold them outside of the fort for the night."

A few minutes later, the herd passed beneath the ridge on which the half-dozen Union soldiers lay in wait for the Confederate patrol.

Just as the fort came into sight, Josh jerked around and stared down over their back trail.

"What's wrong?" Leeboy called out, a frown on his freckled face.

Josh shook his head, keeping his eyes fixed on the trail. "Thought I heard gunshots."

Leeboy glanced over the empty trail, a frown on his freckled face. "I didn't hear nothing. Just your imagination. This drive's got you jumpy as a bit-up old bull at fly time."

The lanky cowboy grunted. He could've sworn he heard gunshots, but then, maybe Leeboy was right. Two weeks of eating dust and smelling cow would make anyone figure they were hearing things. "Suppose you're right."

At that moment, JS, riding point, reined around and

gestured to a small meadow alongside a narrow creek. "Locate'm over there. Water and good graze. I'll ride on into the fort."

Back on the trail, the six Union soldiers slid down the cobbled slope of the limestone ridge to the dead Confederate soldiers sprawled on the ground.

Moving quickly, Lieutenant Tanner barked orders. "Make sure those Johnny Rebs are dead before you try taking their uniforms."

Cautiously, each soldier nudged a motionless body.

"This one's still alive," shouted a young private, Luther Webb, when he rolled one Confederate over. "But just barely."

The dying Confederate opened his eyes slowly, then painfully struggled to reach for his sidearm.

Private Webb squatted quickly and grabbed the soldier's arm. "Sorry, Johnny Reb. Can't let you have that hogleg."

The soldier's eyes hardened, then closed. With a final gasp, he died.

"He's dead now, Lieutenant."

Lieutenant Tanner snapped. "Stop wasting time then, Private. Shuck those blues and get into his clothes."

The young private frowned. "What about the blood on the jacket, Lieutenant? Won't someone notice?"

Tanner fastened his gunbelt about his waist. "Rub dirt on it, and then go bring our horses down from the ridge when you finish, Luther."

The young man nodded. "Yes, sir, Lieutenant."

"You others, take these dead bodies and drag them off the trail. Drop 'em in a gully and cover them best you can. Don't want buzzards bringing anyone from the fort out here until we have the gold."

Sergeant Frank Kincaid shifted the wad of tobacco in his cheek and scratched his grizzled jaw. "What do you think our chances are of pulling this off, Lieutenant?"

Lieutenant Tanner studied Kincaid. The first time he met the sergeant, he knew the man was dangerous. Beside himself, he figured Kincaid was the most dangerous man in this patrol. "It's a long piece to Colorado, Kincaid, but if we keep the gold out of the Confederate's hands, then they won't have the money to support an invasion of Galveston." He hesitated. "That's the glaring deficiency of the Confederate states, Kincaid. They have neither the resources nor funds for a war."

Kincaid frowned. "Huh?"

Tanner lifted an eyebrow, studying his battle-hardened sergeant. "You much of a reader, Kincaid?"

"Reader? Never saw much sense in it," he replied, letting loose a brown arc of tobacco onto the white limestone cobbles at his feet.

With an amused grin on his lips, Tanner replied, "You should. A man can learn a lot from reading. Gold drives a war. In 46 BC, a philosopher named Cicero said 'Endless money forms the sinews of war.' " He paused before adding, "An intriguing concept, Sergeant. Slash the sinews, you lose control."

The burly sergeant just stared at Tanner with a puzzled frown on his face. "Makes no sense to me." He hesitated, then added, "Lieutenant, sir."

Tanner studied him another moment, then shrugged in resignation. "Never mind, Sergeant." He drew a deep breath and stared in the direction of the fort. Nodding slowly, he reminded himself that if he and his men pulled off the hijacking of Confederate gold, the South's sinews would be severed, even if the gold never reached the Union coffers.

He glanced up the cobbled slope at the clatter of hooves. Astride his own pony, the young private led the other horses down the slope. "Here we are, Lieutenant."

Tanner tied his horse to a nearby oak. "All right, boys. Swap saddles with the Johnny Rebs. Some of those crackers at Chadbourne might get suspicious if we rode in on our McClellans."

When he finished, he swung into his saddle and watched as his men carried out his orders.

There was Private Cutch Barstow, the typical career soldier who always tried to find a way to shirk duty. How many times the white-haired old man had been busted in rank was anyone's guess. He loved his whiskey and food as his ample belly demonstrated.

Then there was the sergeant. All Army. Next was Corporal Sam Crocker, another aging career man. And finally, Private Webb, an eighteen-year-old fun-loving boy, and Private Jorge Serra, a Mexican running from the law down in Mexico.

Tanner's thin lips tightened in a cruel smile. For the most part, he had nothing against any of them. They had just been unlucky enough to be selected or foolish enough to volunteer for this mission.

Chapter Two

Two hours later, the small patrol of Union spies camped beneath an outcropping of limestone two miles out of Fort Chadbourne. Lieutenant Tanner reminded them, "We'll ride into the fort in the morning just before the gold arrives. When we do, stay mounted and remember, keep your mouths closed." He patted his breast pocket. "According to orders, we're the Second Texas Cavalry out of Camp Nueces. Our mission is to transport the gold to General John Magruder, the commander of the Confederate District of Texas in Houston."

As one, the soldiers nodded.

Later, the lieutenant reread the orders he had taken from the dead Confederate. So far, all the breaks were going their way, even the orders, which neglected to

9

identify the bearer to the commanding officer at Fort Chadbourne.

The night was clear; the stars were bright; and a soft breeze, cooled by the icy waters of Oak Creek, swept over the camp as the three cowmen squatted around a small fire.

"Going to be a nice day tomorrow," Leeboy drawled, his battered Stetson sitting on the back of his head, revealing tufts of red hair sticking out in all directions like bunches of Johnson grass. "You see the sunset? Red sky at night, cowboy's delight."

Josh shook his head. "You and your silly superstitions, Leeboy. They're just old wives' tales. Like that lucky gold piece you're always rubbing."

Leeboy leaned forward and wagged a finger at him. "Not so. Remember the wart on my thumb? It went away."

Winking at JS Tipton, Josh grunted. "I suppose you're going to claim rubbing it with that chunk of meat and burying the meat is what caused the wart to go away, huh?"

Leeboy arched an eyebrow. "You got a better explanation?" He paused a moment. "See. You don't." He leaned back, shaking his head. "Sometimes I feel sorry for you, Josh. Ignorant of the ways of the world."

With an exasperated sigh, Josh shook his head and sipped his coffee. "What time do we turn the herd over to the soldiers, JS?"

The older man grunted. "Captain Butler said for us

to come in early. He wants to take care of the herd before the gold arrives."

Leeboy whistled softly. "I ain't never seen a hundred thousand dollars in gold. How much do you reckon it weighs?"

"Got no idea, son," replied JS.

"What do you think, Josh?"

"Your guess is as good as mine." He looked at JS. "So the Confederacy plans to use the gold to outfit a couple river steamers with guns, huh?"

"That's what the captain said. 'The Union has got Galveston right now, but we're trying to get it back.' "

Josh arched an eyebrow. "We?"

The older man gave him a wry look. "I know you don't figure this is your war, son, but I reckon when I sell beef to one side, I'm helping them. That makes it 'we.' "

Leeboy grinned and looked from one to the other. He had heard this discussion more times than a church deacon shouts amen.

"Not 'we.' You. Not me," Josh replied. "I work for you, JS. If I don't do my job, I get fired. I didn't drive them critters up here for the South, and I wouldn't do it for the North. I did it because it's my job. Besides, I don't hold with trying to kill off my own kin."

JS shook his head, weary of a discussion that never went anywhere except in circles. "Never mind. Never mind." He groaned as he struggled to his feet. "It's a sin to be getting old and to carry around a belly like this," he said, patting a stomach that hung over his gunbelt. His knees popped when he hobbled over to his bedroll. "Wake me when it's my shift with the beeves," he muttered, slipping between his blankets and laying his head back on his saddle. He pulled his hat down over his eyes.

Josh grinned as he watched the older man settle in for a night's sleep. In the nine years he had worked with JS Tipton, the old man had come to be like a father to him. He glanced at Leeboy and whispered, "Let's let him sleep tonight. This drive's run him down faster than a two dollar watch."

Leeboy nodded to the bedded cattle. "Good enough. They ain't going nowhere tonight. They's worn out more than we are."

Josh chuckled and sipped the last of his sixshooter coffee. "I'll take the first shift."

"Sounds good to me." Leeboy shook his head. "I sure am looking forward to a few glasses of whiskey after we turn them critters over to the Army tomorrow."

Josh nodded, remembering the number of times his old friend had spoken those very words, but failed to stop with a few. More than once, Josh had put a happy, but thoroughly inebriated Leeboy to bed. He rose and swung into the saddle. "I'll wake you later."

Leeboy nodded. He fell asleep as soon as his head hit the saddle.

* * *

Next morning, Josh threw his saddle on his sorrel as the sun eased over the horizon into a cloudless sky. The light southern breeze carried the sweet smell of wild honeysuckle. He shook his head and grinned. Leeboy had been right. *It's going to be a right pretty day.* He swung into the saddle and rode out to the herd where Leeboy and JS waited.

As they started the herd to the corrals behind the livery, a company of Confederate soldiers escorted a large number of civilians from the fort, heading down the trail from which the small herd of beeves had come.

"What's going on over there, JS?" Leeboy nodded to the contingent.

"Union sympathizers. Copperheads," the older man replied. "Couple hundred of them according to Captain Butler, the camp commander. Our boys is taking them to prison down in Austin."

Clucking his tongue and giving his head a brief shake, Josh said, "That's their problem. Let's get these beeves into the corrals."

Far to the west beyond the fort, dust billowed into the clear, warm air.

Private Webb shouted from his perch in the top of the tree from which he had been watching the fort. "Looks like them Butternuts is bringing the gold in, Lieutenant."

"Good job, Luther. Get on back down here. All right, men. You heard him. Mount up and fall in. Keep your mouths closed, but keep your holster unsnapped. I want to get in and out of there as fast as I can."

Just as they moved out, Tanner's dun stumbled. "Blast you," he yelled, jerking the animal's head up. "Watch where you're stepping." The pony took another step and flinched, obviously favoring its front right foot. Tanner muttered a curse. Now he was going to have to switch mounts at the fort, another delay, another chance for their ruse to be discovered.

As Leeboy and Josh herded the beef into the fort, two young boys ran out to the corrals to meet them, intent on helping. Josh waved them away, but Leeboy chided him. "Don't fuss at the boys, Josh. They just want to help. See." He pointed to a barefooted, tow-headed boy throwing open the corral gate. The other youngster crawled up on the opera rail and watched.

"They'll just get in the way."

"Naw, they won't," Leeboy replied good-naturedly.

"Well, if they get themselves hurt, don't go blaming me. Most youngsters their age is always asking for trouble."

Leeboy grinned and shook his head at his partner's impatience with children. Seemed like Josh went out of his way to avoid them, and when Leeboy would scold him about it, the lanky cowpoke would just shrug. "No secret. Just don't care much for children, that's all."

"Hey," Leeboy would respond. "Children, Josh. That's what it's all about." Then he'd wag a finger at his partner and add, "One of these days, I'll find me that pretty little girl and have some children of my own."

And each time, Josh would scoff, "Now, what woman in her right mind would have a broken down, redheaded cowpoke like you?"

With an affable smile and cheerful laugh, Leeboy would respond, "There's someone out there for everyone, partner. Don't ever forget that."

"Not me."

"Yep, even a hard-headed galoot like you."

Absorbed in running the last of the cattle into the corral, Josh didn't notice the patrol entering the fort from the west.

"Okay, son!" shouted Leeboy. "Close the gate. And here," he added, flipping the boy a coin. "Buy you and your friend some licorice." He grinned at his partner when he spotted Josh's raised eyebrows.

The six-man patrol had halted in front of the white limestone building housing the fort headquarters.

"Take a gander, Josh," exclaimed Leeboy. "That must be the fellers with the gold, and look there," he added, pointing to two horses carrying double-rigged sawbuck packsaddles, a dapple-gray and a black. "Reckon that's the gold?"

Four Southern cavalrymen remained in their saddles beside the gray. "Reckon so, Leeboy. The way those soldier boys are keeping their eyes on it, I reckon so."

As they watched, two soldiers untied the packsaddle on the black and then packed it with rations. Leeboy grunted. "The gold must be on the dapple-gray, wouldn't you say?"

Josh chuckled. "I'd say."

At that moment, another patrol rode into the fort, this one from the southeast. "Here comes them boys we spotted yesterday," Leeboy said. "The ones taking the gold back to Houston."

Glancing at the patrol, Josh swung the corral gate closed and slid the lock bar in place. "Glad it's them and not us."

Suddenly, Leeboy shouted, "Josh! Look! Ain't that Zeke out in front of the patrol?"

Josh looked around. He squinted into the morning sun at the erect rider leading in the small cadre of cavalrymen. "Sure looks like it. Let's take us a closer look."

Under his breath, Lieutenant Zeke Tanner whispered over his shoulders as the small patrol drew near headquarters. "Take care, boys. We're going in among the heathens now. Remember what I said, keep your mouths closed."

"What about your horse, Lieutenant? He'll never make it to Colorado," Kincaid asked.

Tanner blew out through his lips. "Got to get another one. Just stay calm."

Suddenly, a voice cut through the clatter of hooves on hardpan. "Zeke! Zeke Tanner!"

Tanner's heart skipped a beat. Behind him came a soft muttering. "Don't do nothing stupid, boys," he said in a harsh whisper, at the same time looking slowly in the direction of the shout.

He uttered a silent curse when he spotted Josh and Leeboy hurrying toward him. Of all times for old friends to show up. He put a grin on his face and waved, at the same time warning his men under his breath. "Stay in formation. I know these two. Just act natural." In a loud voice, he called out, "Patrol, halt."

He guided his limping remount toward his old friends. "Josh, Leeboy! Talk about a sight for sore eyes," he said, reining up and dismounting. For several moments, they shook hands and exchanged greetings. Finally Tanner said, "What are you boys doing out here?"

Leeboy gestured to the corrals. "Selling the Army some beef. What about you? You going to be around awhile?"

"We got to get together," Josh exclaimed. "It's been eight or nine years since we last saw you, you old reprobate. Where you been keeping yourself?"

Tanner hooked his thumb over his shoulder at the patrol. "Doing my part for the South."

Josh grinned and shook his head. "You're still as ugly as ever." He eyed the bars on Tanner's battered shell jacket. "And a lieutenant too. I'm impressed. So, what's your plans for tonight? We just finished our job for the Army, but maybe we can talk our boss into hanging around another day."

Tanner cut his eyes toward the horses in front of headquarters. With a grimace, he replied, "Wish I had time, fellers, but we got orders to escort a shipment to Houston."

"The gold?" Leeboy gestured to the dapple-gray.

Tanner frowned. "How did you know?"

Josh chuckled. "I reckon everybody around here knows about the gold."

A wry grin curled the lieutenant's lips. "Just my luck. But, I sure wish I had time for at least a drink. I don't even have that, boys."

"Shucks." Leeboy frowned. "Wouldn't you know? Where you stationed?"

Tanner remained silent a moment, trying to remember the orders he had read the night before. "Camp Nueces. Down south."

Josh shook his head. "That's a long piece."

With a wry grin, Tanner replied, "Be longer by the time we get back."

At that moment, a Confederate officer stepped onto the porch in front of headquarters. Tanner wheeled around. "Sorry, boys. I've got to report." He studied them a moment longer. "Sure wish we had time to hash up days gone by."

"Me too, Zeke," said Josh, touching his finger to the brim of his Stetson in a parting gesture. "You take care, hear?"

"You too."

The two cowpokes watched as their old friend led his small unit to headquarters and went inside with Captain Butler. The cavalrymen remained in their saddles, saying nothing, looking neither left nor right.

"Those old boys look mighty beat up. Reckon they've seen a heap of fighting," Josh said, taking in the dirty and patched uniforms the patrol wore.

"Good seeing old Zeke," mumbled Leeboy, swinging into his saddle.

"Yep. It was. Too bad he can't hang around a bit."

Leeboy wheeled his pony around and nodded to the saloon. "Well, that ain't going to keep me from a couple drinks of that snake poison they call whiskey hereabouts."

Josh arched an eyebrow. "At ten o'clock in the morning?"

"Why not?"

When Tanner and Captain Butler emerged from headquarters, the lieutenant pointed to his lame pony. "This is the one."

The captain grunted. "Take her over to the livery. Have the corporal swap mounts."

Tanner nodded and saluted, then barked orders. "Remain here, men."

Young Private Luther Webb gulped. Sweat had soaked his shirt under his gray jacket and run down his back he was so scared. Without moving his head, he looked from the corner of his eyes, expecting at any second half-a-dozen Johnny Rebs charging at him with fixed bayonets. He prayed for the lieutenant to hurry.

With every nerve on edge, Tanner waited in the livery as the corporal swapped saddle and tack. Just as the corporal finished, a voice from behind froze Tanner in his tracks.

"Why howdy there, Lieutenant. Didn't reckon I'd see you again."

Tanner spun and faced JS Tipton. "Sorry, old timer. You got the wrong man."

"I'll take your horse outside for you, Lieutenant," said the corporal.

"Fine," Tanner replied, turning to leave.

"Beg your pardon, Lieutenant," the old rancher said. "I thought you was someone else." His eyes flicked over Tanner's tunic, noting the red patch on the elbow of the jacket he was wearing. A frown wrinkled his forehead. Suddenly, he realized what he had discovered. "You ain't the Lieutenant," he said to Tanner's back. "What's going—"

Zeke Tanner spun and slammed the muzzle of his heavy Colt .44 into the old rancher's temple. JS Tipton dropped like a poleaxed steer. In the next second, Tanner spun into a crouch, facing the door and cocking his big Army Colt. No one was around. Quickly, he dragged the unconscious rancher into a stall and covered him with hay.

Taking a deep breath, he straightened his shoulders

and casually strolled from the barn and climbed into the saddle. He saluted the captain smartly, and then, taking his place in front of his men and the gold, he led them from the fort.

A hundred yards out of the fort, Lieutenant Tanner looked back and, as he threw another salute to Captain Butler who was watching from the porch in front of the headquarters, he cautioned his men. "Keep your eyes open, boys. Some old man in the livery knew I wasn't the Johnny Reb lieutenant. I laid him out. I don't know if he's dead or not," he added as he dropped his salute.

Chapter Three

Despite the ninety-plus-degree temperature outside, the saloon was twenty degrees cooler thanks to the thick limestone walls. Josh and Leeboy nursed a whiskey and reminisced their childhood with Zeke Tanner.

Earliest Josh could remember was as toddlers during the Runaway Scrape in 1836 when he, Zeke, and Leeboy rode in a bouncing wagon fleeing Bastrop for Liberty, Texas, just two hoots and a holler ahead of Santa Anna and his Santanistic Army.

After Sam Houston's victory at San Jacinto, the three families returned to Bastrop where the youths grew up together hunting, fishing, farming, and fighting off a mixture of Comanche, Kiowa, and Lipan Apache.

Mentored by an old gimp-legged Cherokee who

taught them the secrets of the forest, the three learned to track like an Indian, even to think like one. The boys could shoot the eye out of a squirrel at a hundred paces, predict the weather from observing the behavior of animals, out-sneak a Lipan Apache, butcher a deer in fifteen minutes, and gentle a wild horse in an hour. Each was as much at home in the wilds of the Texas frontier as an Indian.

"Old Zeke was always the wild one though," Leeboy remarked. "Remember the time Zeke bowed up at Joe Simmons?"

Josh chuckled. "Sure do. We'd worked all day for that old skinflint harvesting his corn. He gave us four bits each."

"Yep. And Zeke pitched a fit. Told the old man that wasn't enough. We should've had a dollar."

"Yep. Just like him. Never could understand why he always figured folks was out to take advantage of him."

Leeboy grew serious. "I don't know if it was as much that or he just figured he was standing up for himself."

Nodding slowly, Josh let his mind wander.

After Comanches murdered Josh's parents when he was sixteen, he drifted, only to learn upon his return the family farm had been sold for taxes. He drifted again, this time accompanied by Leeboy, and the two of them found a home wrangling cattle for JS Tipton near Mason on the edge of the rugged Texas hill country with its limestone cobbles, stunted oaks, and thick cedar.

Leeboy sipped his whiskey. "When was the last time

we seen Zeke, Josh? Was it 'Fifty-five or 'Fifty-six? That was when he had took a job driving a herd to Dodge City."

Josh pondered the question. "Let's see. I was sixteen when the Comanche murdered Ma and Pa. It was about four years later, probably fifty-four."

"Nine years ago." Leeboy shook his head. "Long time."

A young private pushed through the batwing doors, surveyed the saloon, then strode over to the two cowpokes, a look of distress on his face. "You the fellers who rode in with old man Tipton?"

A frown knit Josh's brow. "Yep. What's the matter?"

"Captain Butler wants you all to come over to the infirmary. The old timer got whopped on the head. He's hurt bad, the fort sawbones says."

Leeboy stared at Josh in disbelief, then looked at the private. Distrust edged his words. "Tipton? You talking about JS Tipton?"

"I don't know about them initials. It's the rancher that brought the herd of cattle in. They found him unconscious in the stable. He was all covered up with hay."

Captain Butler met them in front of the infirmary and introduced himself. "You're the cowboys who work for Mister Tipton?"

Josh nodded. "Where is he?"

"In here," the captain said, opening the infirmary door.

A large fireplace took up the middle of one wall. On the opposite wall a half-dozen bunks were evenly spaced. Only one was occupied, the one with JS Tipton.

"He was like that when they found him," the post physician said, his eyes fixed on the slow rise and fall of the old rancher's sunken chest. "He hasn't moved a finger."

Josh grimaced at the old man who had been like a father to him and Leeboy. He looked much older than his fifty-odd years. "What happened? Any idea?"

"Someone struck him a hard blow to the temple with what I believe was a metal object." Blood had turned the white hair around the unconscious man's temple to the color of rust.

Delicately, the doctor parted the stained hair so they could view the cut. "At first I thought someone had used a branding iron, but that wouldn't have made a gash like this. More likely, it was the muzzle of a revolver."

Leeboy cleared his throat. In a soft, strangled voice, he asked, "Is he going to be all right?"

The doctor arched an eyebrow. "Hard to say. He might come around anytime, or—" he hesitated, his voice dropping lower. "Or, he could be like that for days or weeks. Medicine doesn't know much about head injuries like this."

Keeping his eyes fixed on Tipton, Josh spoke in a cold voice. "Who did it?"

Captain Butler shook his head. "No one knows for sure. The livery corporal who found him says when he led Lieutenant Tanner's horse from the barn, the lieutenant and Mister Tipton here stayed behind, talking."

Josh and Leeboy exchanged surprised looks. "Zeke Tanner?"

The captain frowned. "You know the lieutenant?"

"We grew up together," Josh replied, his eyes returning to the old rancher.

Leeboy narrowed his eyes. "Reckon we ought to see what Zeke can tell us, Josh?"

The lanky cowboy considered his partner's question a few moments. He looked around at the captain. "Was there anyone else in the livery?"

"We can find out." The captain stepped to the door and sent the young orderly to fetch the livery corporal.

As soon as the Union patrol had ridden out of sight of the fort, Lieutenant Zeke Tanner kicked their animals into a trot. Five miles farther, he turned the patrol due north from the trail, heading through the middle of the scrub oak forest. "Now shuck those gray coats, men. Put on your blues. We'll change trousers tonight. Private Webb, you and Private Serra hang back just in case someone follows. Don't let them see you."

Sergeant Kincaid rode up beside him, a broad grin on his bearded jaw. "Next stop, La Junta, Colorado, right, Lieutenant?"

Tanner nodded. "As long as the Comanche and Lipan Apache leave us alone and the Johnny Rebs don't figure out what happened any too soon." He hooked his thumb over his shoulder. "Tell the men to keep their eyes moving."

"When do we meet up with our guide?"

Tanner looked around at Kincaid. "Two days. Beyond the Brazos."

"The Brazos. That's a far piece, Lieutenant."

"We'll make it."

"How do we know we can trust this guide, Lieutenant? He's a Injun."

With a sly grin, Tanner nodded. "Gian-nah-tah. The Mexicans call him Cadete. He's a renegade Apache. He knows what the Apache chief, Victorio, or Quanah Parker of the Comanche would do to him if they got their hands on him." His grin broadened. "No way he'll let that happen. You can rest assured, Sergeant, Gian-nah-tah will not betray us."

The livery corporal told his story once again. "I reckon there could have been someone else come in the livery, Captain, but I didn't see them if they did."

Captain Butler looked at Josh. "Seems to me we need to see what Lieutenant Tanner can tell us." He glanced at the Regulator clock on the mantel above the fireplace. "They've been gone four hours. We should be able to catch them by mid-afternoon." He turned to the corporal. "Corporal, take two men and catch the patrol. Inform the lieutenant of the incident and bring back any enlightenment he can shed on the situation."

Forty-five minutes later as the livery corporal and two privates galloped along the patrol's trail, the corporal jerked back on the reins. His remount skidded to a halt.

"What's wrong, Corporal?", said one of the young privates, pulling up beside him.

"Look, over there in the trees. Ain't that one of our jackets?" He pointed to one of the gray shell jackets the Union soldiers had shed.

"Looks like it."

The corporal studied the ground. "There. Their tracks head that way." He looked around to the young private, clearly confused by the course change and the Confederate jacket on the ground. "The patrol turned north here. Houston is back southeast." He frowned at the private. "That's where the patrol was supposed to go."

The young private snorted. "Who knows? Headquarters probably gave them orders to zigzag or something. You know how it is. Nobody knows what the other one is doing. As far as the jacket, it could have been there a long time."

Scratching his head, the corporal considered the private's explanation. "I suppose so." He looked back toward the fort. "Still, maybe I ought to send one of you back to tell the captain about this."

The other private shook his head emphatically. "I ain't riding back alone, not with the Comanche and Apache around. Only three of us out in the middle of this wilderness is scary enough."

Nodding briskly, the second private said, "He's right, Corporal. We best stay together."

For several seconds, the livery corporal pondered their words. "Suppose you're right. If we do run into any Injuns, it'll take all three of us." He dug his heels into his remount. "Let's go, then. Let's catch up with the Lieutenant."

Mid-afternoon, Lieutenant Tanner jerked around at the sound of pounding hooves. Private Luther Webb was racing toward them, leaning low over the neck of his galloping pony. "Johnny Rebs, Lieutenant," he called out. "Coming up from the rear. Serra hid in a patch of oak so he could get behind them."

Private Barstow grabbed for his Spencer cabine. "I'll take care of them."

Tanner barked, "Leave that rifle booted, Barstow! That's an order."

The middle-aged soldier glared at the lieutenant who nodded to Kincaid. "Sergeant, move the men off the trail. Then remove your jacket. We'll wait here for the Johnny Rebs," he said, shucking his blue tunic, tossing it to young Luther Webb. "Better still, you and me'll ride down to meet them." He kicked his horse into a trot to meet the oncoming Confederates.

"What do you have in mind, Lieutenant?"

"What do you think? I just want to be close enough to make sure."

A grin played over Sergeant Kincaid's lips. He unsnapped the flap on his holster. "Yes, sir."

As the two small parties drew close, Tanner held up his hand and reined his pony to a halt. The three Confederate cavalrymen did the same.

Throwing a salute, the corporal said. "Sorry to trouble you, Lieutenant, but—"

He never finished his sentence as the roar of .44 caliber slugs knocked him and his men from their saddles.

"Get down there and make sure they're dead, Sergeant. Then catch up with us. They must have found the old man."

Chapter Four

The infirmary door swung open. Captain Butler stepped inside. He shook his head when Josh looked up at him inquisitively. "No. The patrol hasn't returned yet."

Josh glanced at the clock on the mantle. "It's only eight. Maybe Zeke is pushing them."

Butler glanced at JS. "Maybe. How's Mister Tipton?"

Leeboy ran his tongue over his lips. "About the same," he replied, watching the almost imperceptible movement of the old rancher's chest. "About the same."

"You old boys make it over to the mess hall?"

Josh shook his head. "Don't feel much like eating."

Before the captain could reply, the day orderly rushed in breathlessly. "Captain, come quick. The firewood detail just come in, and they found six of our boys stone-cold dead back on the trail. They brought them back."

Butler brushed past the orderly. "Where are they?"

"Giving their report to the officer of the day at head-quarters," he replied, running after the captain.

Josh and Leeboy frowned at each other. Leeboy glanced at JS. "Why don't you get over there. I'll stay here with JS."

Josh hesitated outside headquarters when he saw the dead bodies, stripped to their red longjohns, in the wood wagon. He grimaced, then hurried inside.

Captain Butler was questioning the two soldiers of the wood detail when Josh entered. "How far down the trail?"

"About five, maybe six miles. They must've been there a spell. Buzzards and animals had got to them pretty good."

"Yes, sir," the other soldier said. "We couldn't leave them lying out there, sir. They was tore up mighty bad."

Butler nodded. "You did right, Private." He turned to the young orderly. "Call the duty sergeant. Tell him to put those boys out there in the infirmary and tell the carpenter we need six coffins." He paused. "And tell the sergeant I want a small patrol ready to ride out first thing in the morning. You two men will accompany me to the site."

He turned to Josh when the orderly and wood detail

left. "You came up that trail yesterday. You see a patrol?"

"Just the one that Lieutenant Tanner brought in this morning."

Agitated, Butler glanced at the Regulator clock. "Where the blazes is that corporal I sent out after Tanner? It's almost nine."

At that moment, the door opened and Leeboy stood staring blankly at Josh. His voice quivered. "JS is dead."

Numbed by the old rancher's death, Josh lay awake in his bunk in the Army barracks until early morning, remembering the last several years on the JS Bar— good years.

"You asleep?" Leeboy's disembodied voice came from the darkness.

"Nope."

"You got the feeling that there's a couple pieces around here that don't fit?"

Josh turned his head on his pillow and stared into the darkness. "You too, huh?"

"Yeah. That patrol old JS talked to yesterday."

"Zeke's?"

"Yeah. They come in this morning, right?" Without giving Josh a chance to reply, he continued. "You and me and JS, we pushed fifty head of cattle to within a couple miles of the fort before sundown, but it took Zeke's patrol all night. Don't that sound odd to you?"

"I'd been wondering the same thing. Of course, their orders might have prevented them from coming straight in. Maybe they were told to arrive this morning."

Leeboy snorted. "You don't believe that, do you?"

"I want to, because if I don't, then—well, I don't like the only other explanation."

The silence grew thick.

In a small voice, Leeboy said, "Me neither."

Several minutes passed. Finally Leeboy blurted out, "I'll never believe Zeke had a hand in it."

His voice taut with resignation, Josh said, "One thing for certain. We'll know tomorrow."

The patrol had not returned by reveille the next morning.

Standing on the porch in front of headquarters, Captain Butler gazed to the southeast. "Could be they run across some hostiles."

Josh shrugged. "That's possible."

Leeboy pulled out a bag of Bull Durham and rolled a cigarette. He tossed Josh the bag. "Maybe they just decided to camp for the night and come in this morning."

"I'll skin them alive if they did," the captain growled. For several more seconds, he stared down the empty trail. Suddenly spinning on his heel, he announced, "I'm going after them."

Josh cleared his throat. "Reckon we'll ride along with you, Captain, if you have no objection."

"No objection. What about Mister Tipton?"

"We've arranged for a wagon, and the carpenter said the coffin would be ready by tonight."

While Josh and Leeboy waited in their saddles for the patrol to form, Leeboy muttered, "Uh oh."

Josh looked around. Leeboy was staring at the sky. He followed his partner's gaze. All he saw was a single crow heading north. "What's wrong?"

"You see that? The crow?"

"Yep. What about it?"

With a hint of trepidation, Leeboy replied, "You know the old saying about when you see crows. One's bad, two's luck, three's health, four's wealth, five's sickness, and six is death." He searched the sky for a second crow, seeing none. Finally, he grimaced, his face solemn. "I got a feeling something's bad wrong."

Shaking his head in feigned disgust, Josh chided Leeboy. "I've told you before. There's nothing to them old superstitions. They're just the ranting of ignorant people."

Leeboy raised his eyebrows. "Say what you want, but you'll see I'm right." He rubbed his right pocket.

Josh chuckled. "That good luck coin sure won't help when you got a dozen or so angry Kiowa on your tail."

Five minutes later as the small patrol made ready to move out, Josh spoke up. "You much of a tracker, Captain?"

"I can get by. What about you?"

He nodded to Leeboy. "All our lives. Learned from an old Cherokee." He pointed to the trail. "It might be best to let me and Leeboy take the point."

Captain Butler studied Josh a moment, then nodded. "It's yours."

They moved out.

A cigarette dangled from Leeboy's lips. Worry etched deep lines in his forehead. "At least we ain't had any rain to wash out the tracks," he muttered, searching the trail ahead of them.

Josh agreed. Although cattle tracks covered the trail, the fresh sign left behind by Zeke Tanner's patrol was obvious, as were the wheel marks left by the wood wagon.

They rode silently, the only sounds the squeaking of saddle leather and the thud of shoed hooves against the hard ground. A mile down the trail, Josh broke the silence. "Take a look," he said, pointing out paw prints in the soft soil at the edge of the trail.

Leeboy chuckled. "Big lobo." He glanced around at the stunted oak and mesquite that stretched as far as the eye could see. "And not long ago either."

"Reckon you're still pretty sharp. But not sharp enough. Look yonder, about a hundred yards west. Standing behind that oak. There he is."

Leeboy grinned when he spotted the large wolf. "Sure enough. Watching us."

As the two looked on, the lobo wheeled and bounded off into the forest.

An hour later, Josh reined up. For a moment, he remained silent, a sinking feeling in his stomach as he studied the shoed horse tracks cutting north off the trail into the forest.

Leeboy pulled over beside Josh, his gaze falling to the trail where Josh's was focused. "Uh oh," he muttered. He shot Josh a look that said I-told-you-so. "I got a bad feeling. You think that's what I think it is?"

Captain Butler reined up. "What's wrong?"

Josh pointed out the sign.

Butler frowned. "What am I looking at?"

Josh and Leeboy exchanged wry looks. "The patrol with the gold, Captain. It turned off here."

Captain Butler looked at him in surprise. "What?"

Josh nodded to Leeboy. "Scout on down the south trail. See if you can find these tracks down there. I'll wager you won't."

"You bet." He wheeled his pony around and headed down the trail, studying the ground carefully.

"Take a look, Captain," Josh said. "See those horse tracks? They're shoed, which means Indians didn't make them."

"Which ones?"

Josh swung from the saddle and squatted to the side of the sign. He swept his arm over the tracks. "All of these." He pointed deep into the scrub forest. "They head north here. And take a look at this set." He pointed to a well-defined imprint. "See how this one is much more distinct? That's because it is a deeper track. I'll wager whatever you want that's the dapple-gray carrying the gold."

Leeboy rode back in. "They're down the trail, Josh. Over the cattle trail and heading toward the fort, which means they were made yesterday morning after we passed with the herd."

"Or the night before."

With a grin, Leeboy nodded. "Or the night before. Now, all the pieces fit."

Josh removed his Stetson and ran his fingers through his sandy hair. "I'm afraid so."

Butler frowned. "I don't understand. Why would Lieutenant Tanner cut north? What pieces?"

"Captain," Leeboy drawled. "Lieutenant Tanner cut north because him and his men just hijacked the hundred thousand dollars in gold."

Captain Butler stared at Leeboy incredulously, his face slack with disbelief. "They what?"

Josh swung back in his saddle. He pointed down the trail. "When we were pushing the herd up the trail, we spotted a Confederate patrol cooking dinner. JS rode over. Leeboy and me were too far to make out any faces."

Leeboy took over. "We pushed the herd up to a couple miles from the fort, but the patrol didn't come in until the next morning."

Butler's forehead wrinkled in a frown.

Josh explained. "A horse moves a heap faster than a herd of cattle. The patrol should have been in the fort before us, even if they'd taken themselves a little siesta after dinner."

Slowly, understanding registered in the captain's face. "You say, Mister Tipton went over and talked to the patrol."

Leeboy nodded. "And according to the livery corporal, JS and Lieutenant Tanner were talking in the livery."

"So Mister Tipton must have known Tanner was not the lieutenant he had talked to on the trail," Captain Butler concluded.

"And Zeke had to knock him out to keep him from exposing them," Josh said, the obvious truth of the words ripping him apart inside.

Butler's frown deepened. "That means Tanner and his men are the ones who ambushed my patrol."

Josh cringed at the words. He couldn't imagine Zeke carrying out such an act, but all of the evidence pointed in that direction. He choked out a reply, as much as he hated the words. "That's the way it looks to me, Captain."

"I thought he was your friend?"

"He was—once. Haven't seen him in nine years or so."

Butler stared north through the scrub forest. His eyes narrowed. He pointed to a gray object some fifty yards deep in the oak and mesquite. "Sergeant. Ride out there and see what that is."

Josh cleared his throat. "Captain, the orders Zeke handed you. Did they mention him by name?"

Butler shook his head. "No names. The orders authorized the patrol to transport the gold."

Moments later, the sergeant returned carrying a Confederate tunic.

Josh and Leeboy frowned at each other.

Leeboy removed his broad-brimmed hat and ran his fingers through a tangle of red hair that looked like kittens had sucked on it. "Well, Josh, what do you think? Outlaw or Copperhead?"

Taking a deep breath and slowly releasing it, Josh chewed on his bottom lip. He remembered JS Tipton lying back at Fort Chadbourne. His blood ran cold. "Either way, we got to go after him."

For several seconds, Leeboy and Josh locked eyes, each reading the determination in the other's, each recognizing the pain the acceptance of their old friend's actions had brought about, each aware of the only choice now remaining for them.

Captain Butler reined his remount around. "Let's get back to the fort. I'll stock you with a week's rations and two men. That's the best I can do. Most of my contingent left yesterday morning taking the other Copperheads to Austin."

Chapter Five

Lieutenant Zeke Tanner pushed his men and animals hard, ignoring the mutters of weariness, pausing only when the animals began to stumble over the rocky soil. His men took their meals in the saddle, hard tack washed down with warm water.

Tanner had been mulling over the possible repercussions if their Apache guide, Gian-nah-tah, learned of the gold—all of them detrimental. So the first night, he rearranged the gold, placing it in the bottom of each packsaddle and placing the rations on top in anticipation of meeting up with their guide. A cursory glance at the open packsaddle would reveal nothing. The weight each animal carried was equal to that of a rider, so there would be no noticeable difference in the depth of tracks.

41

After snugging down the gold and rations, they slept four hours, then continued their journey, taking only short breaks during the day until the next evening. "How far you figure we've come, Lieutenant?" Private Barstow asked as he scratched his ample belly.

Tanner glanced over their back trail. "Hard to say. We pushed mighty hard. I calculate forty miles or so. Another forty will put us near the Brazos. That's where we want to be tomorrow night or the next morning."

Private Barstow grunted. "These old bones are sure getting sore, Lieutenant. When do you figure to stop pushing so hard?"

Tanner studied the older man with a touch of sympathy. Barstow was a career soldier, and still a private, thanks to John Whiskey. Zeke Tanner had decided a year earlier he wasn't about to come to the end of his career as a washed-up lieutenant. And within a few days now, he would realize his goal. "Hold tight, Barstow. A couple more days and maybe we can ease up. Think you can do it?"

Barstow grinned at Corporal Sam Crocker, revealing gaps between rotting teeth. "I suppose if Corporal Crocker can, I can."

Crocker snorted.

Within four hours of discovering their old friend's subterfuge, Josh and Leeboy had returned to the fort, arranged to have JS Tipton carried back to the JS Bar, picked up rations, and with two cavalrymen, Privates Lynde and Howell, ridden back to the point Zeke Tanner had turned his patrol north.

They reined up, staring at Tanner's trail. "Where do you reckon they're headed, Josh?"

Scratching his jaw, the lanky cowpoke gave a brief shake of his head. "Depends. If Zeke's turned outlaw, no telling. Probably just lose himself out there. If he's a Copperhead, I'd figure he'd head to Colorado Territory. I hear that part of the country is pretty much full of Yankee sympathizers."

Leeboy glanced to the west. "Well, we only got an hour or so to track. That's where Zeke's got the advantage."

Private Lynde reined up beside Leeboy. "Advantage, sir?"

Josh nodded. "There's enough Indian in Zeke Tanner to move at night. If I know him, he'll push his men hard, probably give them no more than three or four hours sleep."

The second young cavalryman, Private Howell, spoke. "How do you know that, Mister Miles?"

Josh chuckled. "Call me Josh." He winked at Leeboy. "Because, Private, me and this red-headed jasper here grew up with Zeke Tanner down near Bastrop, just below Austin. The three of us ran through the woods like wild Indians ourselves."

"Yep," Leeboy put in. "Old Zeke, he's doing just what I'd do or what Josh would do. Move at night."

Wheeling his bay about, Josh heeled him into a trot. "Then I reckon we best stop chewing the leather and get to work. We got an hour of good light. We ought to pick up a few miles."

At the end of the first two miles, Leeboy grinned crookedly at Josh. "He's doing it."

Josh grunted. "I figured he would. Zigzagging. He didn't forget."

Later, around a small fire, Private Lynde asked, "How far do you reckon we've come, Mister—I mean, Josh?"

"We moved at a fair pace. What do you think, Leeboy? Six, eight miles?"

Leeboy nodded. "About that." He winked at the young privates. "Tomorrow, we'll pick up a heap more than that, ain't that right, Josh?"

The lanky cowboy nodded. "A heap. So, you best turn in. We're riding out at first light."

Private Lynde cleared his throat. "I noticed the trail sort of zigzagged, Josh. Why is that? Don't they know where they're going?"

Chuckling, Josh replied, "You bet he knows. Zeke Tanner is almost Indian. He zigzags so if we lose the trail, we have to cast about. We don't know when he's going to zig or zag. If he went in a straight line, and we lost it, all we'd have to do is keep riding, and we'd stumble across it." He shook his head and winked at Leeboy. "Yep, Private. Zeke Tanner knows exactly where he's going."

Next morning, they rode out just after false dawn burned away. The sign was so obvious that between Leeboy and Josh, the small party followed it at a mile-eating lope.

Leeboy and Josh rode side-by-side. "Where do you reckon Zeke is about now?"

Josh said, "I figure old Zeke is closer to the Brazos than he is us, but if we keep pushing, maybe we can close the gap."

Just before noon, Josh and Leeboy reined up at the dead ashes of Tanner's camp the previous night. "We're closing in," Leeboy announced, nodding at the sign.

"Uh oh," Josh exclaimed.

"What?"

"Look at the trail leaving camp. What do you see?"

Leeboy studied it. A slow grin played over his lips. "He switched the gold to both pack animals."

Josh frowned. "He ought to know that won't throw us off."

"Reckon so." Leeboy tilted his Stetson forward and scratched the back of his head. "Why do you suppose he did something like that?"

"No idea." The lanky cowpoke gazed north along the trail. "But, one thing is for certain."

"What's that?"

"We'll find out sooner or later."

Lieutenant Zeke Tanner pushed hard all day, and that night, he followed the routine of the previous one—four hours sleep, then back on the trail. "We can rest when we reach La Junta," he told them the second night. "We'll hit the Brazos in the morning and just beyond, meet up with our guide."

Just after sunrise the next morning, Tanner and his patrol waded the ankle-deep water of the Clear Fork of the Brazos River. He paused on the north shore and studied the countryside. Great oaks and ancient pecan trees lined either side of the river.

Sergeant Kincaid pulled up beside him. His eyes reflected his weariness. "How are we doing, Lieutenant?"

Tanner pointed northwest. "There's a small hill an hour's ride in that direction. We're scheduled to meet Gian-nah-tah at noon today. We'll rest here a couple hours, Sergeant. Lay a fire. The men deserve hot coffee." Had the lieutenant known the repercussions of that decision, he would never have made it.

The weariness among the Union cavalrymen vanished.

While the coffee was boiling, the men unsaddled their remounts, watered them, put them out to graze, and then jumped in the shallow river, clothes and all.

For a few short minutes, they forgot about the war and
frolicked like boys in a swimming hole back home.

Later, as they lay dozing on their blankets, Private
Serra, who had been given guard duty, rushed into the
camp. "Lieutenant! A wagon. She comes this way. *El
hombre viejo, hombre joven, y mujer joven.* An old
man, young man, and young woman."

Lieutenant Tanner leaped to his feet, his Army Colt
appearing magically in his hand. His men rolled from
their blankets, grabbing for Colts and Spencers. "Find
some cover, boys. Who are they, Serra?"

The Mexican shrugged. "Nothing to fear, I think,
Lieutenant. Just people, common ones." He nodded to
the approaching Conestoga. When the old man driving
spotted the patrol, he veered in their direction. A blond-
haired young woman sat on the seat beside him, and a
young man about the woman's age forked a spirited bay
alongside the wagon.

Kincaid sidled up beside Tanner and muttered,
"What are your orders, sir?"

Tanner's brain raced. "On the outside chance we've
shaken any pursuit, we can't afford to have anyone tell
the Graybacks where we are."

Kincaid glanced at him in surprise, then grimaced,
puckering his brow. "I understand the men, but a
woman?"

For several moments, Tanner remained silent, cursing the old man for driving up on them. Why couldn't

he have hit the river a mile or so on either side? The fool! He had left Tanner with no choice. "Not the woman. We'll have to take her with us."

"Excuse me for saying so, Lieutenant, but that's trouble." Kincaid eyed the men about him. "Bad trouble."

Keeping his eyes on the approaching wagon, Tanner snapped. "That's my problem, Sergeant." He cursed himself for taking a break and making camp instead of moving on. Had they continued their flight, they would never have encountered the wagon.

"Yes, sir." Kincaid nodded and eased around to the side.

"Whoa there, boys," shouted the old man to his horses, pulling his four-up to a halt outside of camp. "Howdy, gents," he called out. "Don't mean to intrude. Name's John Terry. This here's my daughter, Emmeline, and my boy, Matthew. We're heading down to Mason. Bought us a small ranch."

Lieutenant Tanner nodded, a grin on his face. "Got hot coffee. You're welcome to some."

John Terry made no effort to climb down from the wagon. "Much obliged, but we ate a few hours back. Mighty hospitable of you, but we need to be pushing on though it is right nice to see smiling faces."

Kincaid glanced at Tanner who sensed the question in his sergeant's look. For long seconds, Zeke Tanner struggled with his conscience. What if John Terry did give Tanner's position away? What about the gold?

He tilted the muzzle of his Colt.

John Terry's eyes grew wide with the sudden comprehension of what was to take place. Before he could shout, Zeke Tanner blew the back of the old man's head off. In the next second, Kincaid killed Matthew Terry.

Emmeline Terry screamed.

She was still screaming as they threw her on her brother's bay and continued their desperate flight to Colorado.

Josh reined up when he spotted the tree line of the Brazos, a snake-like green line on the horizon. "There's the river, boys. Shuck those Spencers and keep your eyes open." He studied the sign they had been following. He pointed to the northwest. "Looks to me they're heading toward that dead oak on the yonder side of the river. What do you think, Leeboy?"

The red-headed cowpoke removed his hat and ran his fingers through his hair as he studied the trail that seemed to be leading directly toward the lightning-killed oak, the skeletal branches of which clawed the air like witch's fingers. "Yep," he muttered. "It do." He pointed east. "So I reckon we best cut the river yonder to the right, then move up through the trees."

Josh grinned.

"What?" Leeboy frowned. "You don't think so?"

"Oh, no," the lanky cowboy quickly replied. "I was thinking the same thing."

"Then what's the grin for?"

"Not much. I was thinking how you and me always

thought so much alike. Like they say long-time married folks do except you're a heap uglier than any woman."

Leeboy shot back. "Well, you ain't no prizewinner for a man neither."

Behind them, the young privates frowned at each other.

Despite the morning heat, Josh shivered as they slowly made their way upriver in the cool shade cast by the canopy of leaves high overhead. Off to his left, the shallow, clear water of the Brazos rippled past with a soft, musical tone.

The four riders had spread into a skirmish line and were slowly walking their ponies through the trees. From the corner of his eyes, Josh spotted Leeboy patting the pocket where he kept his lucky gold eagle. Keeping his eyes moving, quartering the shadows ahead, he muttered, "Reckon that piece works for both us?"

"Didn't think you believed in superstitions," Leeboy muttered gruffly, keeping his eyes moving.

"Don't, but at a time like this, I'll take any help I can get."

Leeboy chuckled. Suddenly, he fell silent. "Josh," he whispered. "Up yonder to the left. A wagon."

"Hold it, boys," Josh ordered under his breath. "Let's see what we can see." He moved his bay behind the thick bole of a pecan and peered around the trunk.

"Nothing moving," whispered Private Howell, licking his dry lips and swallowing the lump in his throat.

"Let's go in slow, boys. Keep your eyes moving."

Slowly, they eased forward.

Without warning, Private Lynde shouted, "Look! There's two men laying yonder. They ain't moving either."

Chapter Six

As they packed the dirt over the two lonely graves, Leeboy stepped back and shook his head. His voice reflected his disbelief. "I know why Zeke did it, Josh, but Lord alive, I never figured he was that cold-blooded."

Josh lifted his gaze from the two graves, the sadness in his eyes evident. He shook his head. "This isn't the Zeke Tanner we knew, Leeboy. This Zeke might be a Copperhead or an outlaw, but the old Zeke we grew up with wouldn't kill nobody like this."

For several seconds, Leeboy grimaced, the freckles on his gaunt face running together in one big blotch. "I reckon you're right, but he didn't kill the girl. At least, that's what the signs read."

Josh looked around at the two young privates watching him. "No, he didn't do that, but that gives him a hostage."

He paused a moment. Staring back down at the graves, he removed his hat. After a few seconds, he tugged it back on, and looked around at the four horses standing quietly in harness in front of the Conestoga, staring curiously at him. From their height, which was over sixteen hands, and their conformation, they were a Percheron cross, although none of the four approached the seventeen hundred pounds of a pure-blood Percheron. "Unhitch the horses, boys. Give them a chance." He swung into the saddle. "And be quick about it. We've let Tanner get another hour ahead. Catch up with us." And he wheeled his bay about and set out on the trail of Lieutenant Zeke Tanner, hatred and vengeance now burning in his chest.

Just as the hill on which he was to meet Gian-nah-tah and his followers came into sight, Lieutenant Tanner jerked around as Private Luther Webb raced up to him, shouting, his excited words running together. "Lieutenant, Lieutenant! They're coming, they're coming! The Butternuts! I saw them! They're coming!"

At the young man's words, the patrol started to rein up, but Tanner kept them going. "Kick your ponies into a fast lope, boys. We can't hold back." He motioned Private Webb to fall in beside him. Above the pounding of hooves, he shouted, "Now, what did you see, boy?"

The young man's face was red with excitement. His Adam's apple bobbed. "Through the eyeglasses, Lieutenant. Three or four miles back, four men. Two cowboys and two soldiers. Butternuts."

Tanner felt his blood chill. Two cowboys! Who else? Josh Miles and Leeboy Strauss. He muttered a curse under his breath. What else could go wrong? He nodded and, to hide his own consternation, gave the private a grin. "You did fine, Luther. Now fall back a piece and keep an eye on them."

Private Webb saluted and returned to drag.

Sergeant Kincaid spurred his remount up beside Tanner. He shifted the wad of tobacco into his cheek. "We got a problem, Lieutenant?"

Tanner kept his eyes forward, his jaw set. "No problem." His eyes narrowed as he studied the hill on which he was to meet their guide. A cruel grin twisted his lips as he decided what to do about Josh and Leeboy. "No problem at all. I know exactly what needs to be done."

When the patrol approached the crest of the hill, half-a-dozen Indians emerged from the cedar and mesquite. Tanner identified the Comanche by the intricate patterns in their warshirts, the Apache by their knee-high leggings and gaudy headbands, and Kiowa by their deerskin shirts and deerskin caps with religious symbols. All wore loincloths.

Tanner halted the patrol just as Kincaid slapped for his sidearm, but Tanner cautioned him. "Be easy, Sergeant. Easy. Remember what I told you. They're renegades. They want money, not scalps."

Reluctantly, Kincaid dropped his hand from the butt of his sidearm. "I sure hope you know what you're doing, Lieutenant. I truly do."

"So do I." He glanced around at his patrol. As one, they nervously surveyed the oncoming Indian party. "But, to be on the safe side, men, unsnap your holsters. These heathen might have got word about the gold, and if they did, they'll slit our throats without a second's hesitation."

Her hair falling down over eyes red from tears, Emmeline Terry bit her lips. She struggled to stifle her sobs. Under his breath, Tanner warned her, "Stop that crying. Do what I say if you want to live."

A muscled warrior, his dark face a mask of scars and his knotted fist grasping a Henry repeater, rode forward. He held up the Henry in a sign of peace. Cold black eyes beneath a red Apache headband peered deep into Tanner's, searching for weakness. His lips twisted cruelly. "You Tanner?"

With every nerve on edge, Lieutenant Zeke Tanner rode up to meet the warrior. "Gian-nah-tah?" He quickly scanned the party behind the large Apache. His pulse raced. He'd come too far to permit a band of vermin-infested Indians to stop him. He narrowed his eyes. "You were to come alone, but you have many warriors." His tone was accusing.

A faint smile played over the Apache's lips, and the look in his eyes was of a fox ready to pounce on a prairie hen. "Me and my warriors, we ride together. Comancheria does not welcome outsiders." His reply resonated with smug defiance.

A faint smile curled Tanner's lips. "I am pleased Gian-nah-tah is so wise."

The giant Apache's smug grin faded into a puzzled frown.

Tanner continued, turning his saddle and nodding to the valley below. "Soon four men will ride into the valley. They want to stop us from reaching Palo Duro Canyon." He turned back to Gian-nah-tah. "There is gold hidden there, gold buried by the Graybacks."

Kincaid shot Tanner a startled look, but the lieutenant continued. "Gian-nah-tah, you and me and my men go." He gestured to the warriors. "They stay. Kill those who follow. When we reach Palo Duro, because of your help, I will share the gold with you and your warriors."

The giant warrior's face twisted in shrewd concentration. He eyed the packsaddles on the two horses. "Maybe gold is there, maybe?"

Tanner nodded sharply. "No. That is only our rations. I do not lie. The gold is hidden at Palo Duro."

Gian-nah-tah studied him suspiciously.

Keeping his eyes on the Apache, the lieutenant called over his shoulder. "Barstow!"

The middle-aged cavalryman rode forward. "Yes, sir, Lieutenant."

"Get Gian-nah-tah and his men a twist of tobacco."

The heavily muscled warrior watched keenly as Barstow fumbled with the ropes on a packsaddle, pulled aside the canvas covering, and dug through the rations for the twist of tobacco that looked like a short piece of brown manila rope. "Here you are, Lieutenant."

Tanner nodded to Gian-nah-tah. "Give it to our friend here." A faint grin played over his lips.

Gian-nah-tah savagely tore off a piece, then tossed it to his followers. He peered over the patrol's back trail. As he did, a small band of riders appeared on the far side of the valley below. Instinctively, the warriors backed their ponies into the cover offered by the cedars.

Tanner glanced over his shoulder. "Those are the ones," he said. He paused, then demanded in a tone edged with insult, "So will the great Gian-nah-tah's warriors fight? Or hide?"

The Apache renegade's dark eyes blazed, then cooled. "How much gold?"

Zeke Tanner knew the warrior would ask such a question. He replied. "Enough to buy the finest rifles, to buy much ammunition, and to supply yourself with enough good whiskey to last the winter."

The warriors behind Gian-nah-tah yelped in delight and anticipation. For several seconds, the massive warrior studied Tanner. Finally, he nodded. "I will guide you. They remain. But," he added, a veiled threat in his voice, "you will be wise not to forget your promise of the gold."

A broad-shouldered warrior rode up to Gian-nah-tah. One eye drooped, and he wore a cruel grin on his lips. He whispered to the Apache and pointed to Emmeline.

Gian-nah-tah's eyes glittered. He grunted. "Walk-in-Sky wants to buy woman."

Emmeline gasped. She pressed her fists to her lips

and stared in wide-eyed shock at the warrior, then cut her horror-filled eyes to Tanner.

Tanner gave his head a single shake. "She is mine," he replied softly, but firmly.

Walk-in-Sky spoke to Gian-nah-tah, whose grin grew wider as he relayed the warrior's offer. "He will give two hundred dollars in gold coin."

For several seconds, Zeke Tanner studied Walk-in-Sky. "She is my woman," he repeated without inflection.

Walk-in-Sky glared at Tanner, and then with a savage jerk on the reins, yanked his pinto around and returned to the warriors milling about on the crest of the small hill.

"You make enemy," Gian-nah-tah said.

Tanner grinned. "I have many enemies, but I still live."

The challenge in his tone was not lost on the Apache warrior whose lips quivered in an amused smile.

"Have your warriors follow us over the hill. Then I'll tell you what to do."

The muscular warrior barked his orders. His followers obeyed. He looked around at Tanner, then his dark eyes slid over to the packsaddle. His eyes narrowed, and a crooked grin curled his lips.

Kincaid sidled up next to Tanner and whispered under his breath. "I hope you know what you're doing, Lieutenant. They ain't dumb. Sooner or later they'll figure out where the gold is."

Tanner smirked. "Not if they're dead. Why do you

think I want them to ambush Josh and Leeboy? Maybe they'll kill each other off."

"You think they will?"

"Maybe those Graybacks and the renegades, but not Josh and Leeboy. They got too much Indian in them to fall for it."

For a moment, the sergeant studied Lieutenant Tanner. "What about that one?" He nodded to Gian-nah-tah.

"That one would slit his own mother's throat for gold. When he learns he can have their share, he'll be happy as a hog wallowing in a mudhole." What Tanner left unsaid was that when the Apache warrior was no longer needed, he'd be eliminated, along with a few others.

Leeboy shouted and pointed to the crest of the hill. "There they are, Josh. Going over the top. They got some reinforcements. Indians!"

As soon as Josh spotted their quarry, he forgot about the gritty dust burning his eyes and the pungent stink of horse sweat stinging his nostrils. Now he knew why Zeke had split the gold between the two pack animals. It was an effort to mislead the Indians. "Another hour and we'll have them."

Chapter Seven

As soon as the Union patrol dropped below the crest of the hill, Tanner reined up. He gestured to the cedar on either side of the trail.

"Have your warriors hide in the cedar. When those who follow come over the hill, your men will attack," the lieutenant explained. "When your warriors finish, they can catch up with us."

Gian-nah-tah barked orders, and the five renegade Indians vanished into the cedar.

Josh clenched his teeth and drove his bay hard. At the base of the small hill, he leaned forward in his saddle, pressing his feet into stirrups. Halfway up the hill, he reined up. "Hold it, boys."

Leeboy jerked his pony aside to keep from running

into Josh. With sweat running down his gaunt cheeks, he called out, "What's wrong?"

Josh studied the top of the hill some two hundred feet above. "I don't like riding into something I can't see. Zeke had to spot us coming across the valley." He nodded to the crest of the hill. "I wouldn't put it past him to arrange a surprise for us, would you?"

A sly grin spread over Leeboy's flushed face as he realized what Josh was suggesting. "No, sir, I certainly would not put it past him. Probably as soon as we came over the top."

"You take Lynde and go around to the west. Howell and me will go east. If anyone is waiting, we'll come up behind and below them."

Leeboy drew his Colt and nodded. He patted the gold coin in his pocket. "Pat it once for me," Josh said with a crooked grin. He looked around at Private Howell. "Cock that Spencer, son, and come up beside me. I don't want you to get excited and shoot off my hat. It cost me half-a-month's pay back in Mason."

The young private blushed. "Don't you worry none. Back home in East Texas, I brought down squirrels with one shot."

Cedar grew thick on the side of the hill, forcing them to take a meandering course. Josh rode slowly, warily, stopping every few moments to listen. From time to time, the bay's hoof clattered on rock, causing his pulse to flutter.

Their course slowly changed from east to north as

they circled the hill. They had seen nothing, heard nothing out of the ordinary. The hot, still day was suffocating. Private Howell sucked in a deep draught of air.

"Scared?" Josh whispered.

"Yes, sir."

"Me too."

From the corner of his eyes, Josh saw the young man glance around at him.

"I don't feel so bad now," the private whispered.

Another fifty feet and they began turning back to the west. Suddenly, Josh reined up and motioned for silence. He pointed up the hill.

From somewhere above came a soft gurgling, a faint fluttering noise. Josh recognized the sound immediately. On several occasions, he had been around horses with breathing problems. The sounds were identical.

Neither Leeboy's nor Private Lynde's horses had exhibited the problem, which could mean only one thing. There was a strange horse not far away, and chances were the strange pony was carrying an Indian.

Josh looked inquiringly at Private Howell, who nodded that he also heard the sound. Touching a finger to his lips, they eased up the hill toward the sound.

A brittle silence that oozed tension filled the air. Suddenly, the crack of a rifle followed instantly by the roar of handguns shattered the stillness. The entire hillside erupted in gunfire and war cries.

Josh slammed his heels into his pony's flanks and, leaning over his bay's neck, charged through the cedar.

He burst from the cedar into a small clearing in which two startled Indians were wheeling their ponies around and bringing their rifles up to fire.

Without lessening his speed, he fired twice, knocking one of the warriors from the saddle and grazing the other's shoulder. As he swept past the second Indian, Josh caught a sidelong glance of the warrior swinging the muzzle of his rifle around to Josh's back. A second rifle cracked, and the warrior tumbled from the back of his pony.

As suddenly as it had begun, the encounter was over.

Josh reined about and saw the taut face of Private Howell, smoke wafting from the muzzle of his Spencer. "Much obliged," Josh said with a grin, nodding at the dead warrior.

The young man gulped. His face grew pale. He stared at the dead warrior. "I–I never kilt no one before, not even an Injun."

"Comanche," Josh said. "You did what you had to do, son. If you hadn't got him, he would've got me."

"Josh! You two all right?" Leeboy's voice carried above the cedar.

"Over here. We got two."

"Need help here. Lynde caught a bullet. Both our ponies are down."

"Busted his leg," Leeboy said from where he was squatting beside the grimacing young soldier, when Josh and Private Howell rode up. A few feet beyond lay a dead Indian. The freckle-faced cowboy nodded to the second Indian, who was sprawled beneath a cedar. "Kiowa. One got away. Comanche."

"Don't worry," Josh said, reloading his Colt. "We'll catch 'em, but first, we need to take care of this young feller."

"He can't go on." Leeboy had cut away the pants leg and was inspecting the wound. "It's busted up pretty bad. All we can do is clean it up, set it best we can, then send him back."

"That'll be a slick trick, us with only two horses," Josh said. He glanced up at Private Howell. "See if you can pick up a couple of those Indian ponies while we take care of business here."

Leeboy rolled up his sleeves. "Wish we had hot water." He nodded to the canteen dangling from his saddle horn. "But, that'll have to do."

Josh chuckled and glanced at the sun. "It's so blasted hot, I reckon the water will be warm enough."

Within an hour, they had cleaned and dressed the wound, then set the leg. That was when Private Howell rode in, shaking his head. "The horses must've taken off like turpentined cats. I couldn't find hide nor hair of them."

Josh grimaced and glanced north after Zeke and the gold. "Then we'll have to ride double back to the river and hope the horses we turned loose this morning haven't drifted too far."

Leeboy lifted an eyebrow.

"I know," Josh said. "He's getting farther away, but we'll catch up."

Two hours later, they reached the wagon where the wounded private was placed in the bed and Private Howell set about building a fire. The draft horses were nowhere to be seen. "Head upriver," Josh said, cursing their luck under his breath. He couldn't remember the last time so many things had gone wrong. "I'll go down."

An hour later, he spotted the horses grazing peaceful-ly at the edge of the tree line. He uncoiled his rope and shook out a loop and let it hang at the side of his bay.

The unconcerned horses looked up as he slowly approached. "At least they're not spooky," he muttered, drawing closer.

The large animals stood motionless, permitting Josh to ride up beside the first one, a dun with a blaze on its forehead, and gently drop the loop over its head. He clucked. "What a shame," he said, tightening the loop while admiring the horses. "I sure hate to leave fine animals like you out here."

He headed back to the wagon, leading the dun. To his surprise, the other three fell in behind.

The sun had set by the time Josh reached the wagon. The small fire was a welcome sight. He tied the dun to a wagon wheel and squatted for a cup of coffee.

He retrieved a small packet of folded documents from his shirt pocket and handed them to Private

Howell. "I took these from the old man before we buried him. It identifies him and his boy. Their name's Terry. Tell Captain Butler that Tanner has the girl. We'll bring her back if we can."

Howell nodded. "What about the wagon? You reckon we should take it back? Probably be an easier ride for Lynde."

Leeboy cut his eyes toward Josh who shrugged. "Up to you. You think you can handle a four-up?"

The young private grinned broadly. "Can I? Why, I cut my teeth on them back home." He nodded emphatically. "Yes, sir. I can handle them. Besides, I hate to see fine animals like these left out here for mountain lions and wolves."

Josh rose to his feet and drained his coffee. "That being the case, I reckon we'll leave you boys now. Take our rations. We'll pick up those on your ponies back at the hill."

Private Lynde frowned. "You're leaving tonight?"

Josh swung into the saddle. "We'll spend the night at the hill. This way we'll make up an hour or so of what we lost."

Lynde's pale face twisted in regret. "Sorry I was so much trouble, Josh." He glanced at his leg. "I—"

"Trouble? Why boy, you weren't no trouble at all. In fact, I reckon Leeboy and me would be tickled to ride the river with you anytime."

"Yes, sir," Leeboy put in as he climbed into his saddle. "Anytime at all."

Chapter Eight

Maintaining the same grueling routine, Tanner rode until late in the night, then made camp. Gian-nah-tah and his remaining warrior, the Comanche, Black Fox, rode ahead to scout their trail. The Apache had pointed out the Big Dipper to Tanner before he left. "When stars face down, I return."

Emmeline Terry was exhausted. Ignoring the hungry looks cast in her direction, she sat at the base of a scrub oak, wrapped her arms around her knees, which she drew up to her chest, laid her head on them, and closed her eyes.

Private Jorge Serra elbowed Corporal Crocker and nodded to the young woman. He grinned lecherously and licked his lips. Suddenly, the crisp click of a cocking hammer broke into his carnal thoughts.

67

Cold words froze the lust stirring in him.

"I swear by the Lord Almighty I will kill the first yahoo who touches the woman."

Serra looked around into the muzzle of Zeke Tanner's Colt six inches from his forehead.

"Do you understand, Private?"

Serra gulped. "Yes, sir. *Cuando Dios es mi testigo, yo no toco a mujer.* As God is my witness, I not touch woman."

Keeping his eyes fixed on the Mexican, Tanner spoke loudly. "Did everyone hear what I said?"

Only when they answered did he lower his Colt, spin it once on his finger, and pop it back in its holster. When he looked around, Emmeline Terry was staring up at him, her face a mixture of disbelief and gratitude. He wanted to smile at her, to assure her she had nothing to fear, but he couldn't. Besides, she wouldn't believe him, not after he murdered her brother and father.

Turning on his heel, Lieutenant Zeke Tanner moved from the firelight into the darkness. He stared at the stars overhead, fighting bitter self-recrimination for killing the two men. It was a job that had to be done, he told himself in an effort to assuage his guilt. He couldn't have afforded the outside chance that Terry would inadvertently give them away. Tanner muttered a soft curse. If only he had not given the order to make camp back at the river.

He glanced at his men squatting around the fire, envying their responsibility to simply carry out orders instead of having to give them. Tanner drew a deep breath. He needed to get over feeling sorry for himself. Especially if he wanted to carry out his plan to its fruition.

His big problem was Josh and Leeboy. If they weren't dead, and he would have bet his own life they weren't, they were bound to catch him long before he reached Palo Duro Canyon, the Spanish name for 'hardwood,' the trees that grew in the canyon. He had to delay his old friends, at least for a couple of days.

Once he reached the canyon, he could elude anyone, even the Comanches who made the canyon their home. He had personal knowledge of tunnels that stretched for miles, tunnels filled with hazards that would quickly kill the unwary and aid those familiar with its dangers.

Because of his own plan, he had said nothing when Gian-nah-tah, instead of zigzagging as Tanner had done, guided them on a direct northerly course. That and the help of Gian-nah-tah's remaining warrior, Black Fox, could be the ruse to throw Josh off his trail.

He strode back to the fire and called Sergeant Kincaid aside. He led the way beyond the firelight to a copse of scrub oak where he expressed his concerns of their pursuit to Kincaid, concerns that surprised the sergeant. Officers just gave orders. They never explained them. "Why are you telling me this, Lieutenant?"

"Because as long as we have that gold, those two jaspers will stick to us like two coats of paint. We've got to create a subterfuge."

Kincaid frowned. "A sub–what?"

Tanner resisted a smile. "A trick." He glanced up at the Big Dipper. "Gian-nah-tah won't be back for another hour, so, here's what we'll do. First, put the gold in the saddlebags. There's five of us, so the additional weight won't bother our horses too much. Then we'll pack all the rations in one packsaddle, and the other, fill it with rocks. And do it before Gian-nah-tah and Black Fox return."

"Rocks?" The sergeant's frown deepened.

"I know Josh Miles." A satisfied grin settled over his face. "I'll send Private Serra and Black Fox to the east with the rocks. We'll continue north. He won't have a choice. He'll have to follow the deepest tracks, thinking it is the gold." He paused. "Any questions?"

Kincaid had to admit the idea, while chancy, just might give them the time they needed to reach La Junta and the Union forces. "Just one. How can you be certain he'll follow Serra?"

"He's good, real good. Leeboy too. We'll wipe out Serra's and Black Fox's tracks where they head out. Josh will follow us north."

Kincaid frowned, confused. "I thought you didn't want him to follow us?"

Tanner's grin grew wider. "The one sign that kept them on our trail at first was the deep tracks of the horse carrying the gold. Those two are good enough trackers that they probably figured out we split the gold between two animals, and chances are, now they've spotted the Indians, they know why. As soon as they discover three horses are missing, and all of the tracks are the same, they'll guess we're trying to snooker them. Believe me," he added, "they won't have a choice. They'll be forced to come back to this camp and cast around. They'll cut Serra's tracks. And they'll spot the deeper prints."

The frown faded from Sergeant Kincaid's face. "That's pretty slick, Lieutenant. Pretty slick. If it works."

Tanner chuckled. "It will. Those two jaspers are too good at reading sign for it not to work. Any more questions?"

"No, sir. No more."

"Good. Let's get to it. The sooner we get the gold to La Junta, the sooner we can get back in the real war," he said with a sly grin.

They headed back to the fire. As they did, a dark figure rose from the grass and peered after them. A cruel grin twisted Gian-nah-tah's lips. So, the lieutenant had lied. There was no gold at the canyon of hardwood because the patrol was carrying the gold. Hurrying back to where Black Fox waited, he decided to keep what he had learned a secret.

An hour later when Gian-nah-tah and Black Fox rode into camp, Tanner explained that he wanted to create a false trail for those pursuing. "When they head east, we'll wipe out their tracks for a short piece."

The muscular Apache feigned a frown. Quickly, Tanner explained what he had in mind. A look of understanding came over Gian-nah-tah. "We do as Tanner asks."

Well before sunrise, the parties split, Black Fox and Private Serra leading the packhorse carrying the rocks due east. "Ride into the night, Private. In two days, turn the horse loose and catch up with us. Black Fox will guide you."

Tanner and Kincaid erased the tracks leaving the camp and headed north, with Sergeant Kincaid assigned the responsibility of looking after Emmeline Terry.

Josh and Leeboy moved out with the sun. They followed the sign at a lope, eating up the miles, drawing ever closer to their quarry. A few times, the ground proved too hard to hold sign, but each time, they found it once again some distance to the north.

"This ain't Zeke's trail. He don't travel like this in a straight line," Leeboy said. "I reckon he's got one of them Indians leading the way."

Josh nodded. "Yep. I noticed that. Zeke zigzags. I don't understand what he's up to unless he don't want to waste time going back and forth."

Mid-afternoon, Tanner spotted the caprock, the Llano Estacado rising sharply to five hundred feet above the woodland in which they journeyed.

The Llano Estacado, the Staked Plains, was a treeless, flat plateau stretching from Central Texas north to the Canadian River Valley and east to the Pecos River Valley, a dry, hostile area larger than all of New England—all controlled by Apache, Comanche, and Kiowa.

Alternating layers of red soil, white calcium, yellow, gray, and lavender mudstone made up the rugged incline to the Staked Plains.

Gian-nah-tah had explained they would not ride on the plains, but follow the caprock from below.

Just before they reached the rugged incline, a band of Kiowa attacked in two waves astride galloping warhorses.

With the first shot, Gian-nah-tah led the patrol into the water-slashed gullies in the slopes of the caprock.

"Shoulda knowed things had been too peaceful," Private Barstow grumbled as he dropped behind a chest-high ridge of calcium and threw his Spencer to his shoulder.

Corporal Crocker grinned and spit out a stream of tobacco. "Me, I been bored," he said, touching off a shot. "Send all them heathens you want at me. With my little Spencer here, I can load on Sunday and shoot all week." He shouted above the clamor of gunfire. "How you doing, Luther?"

Luther Webb was too frightened to speak, and too frightened not to keep firing as fast as he could.

Smoke from the black powder cartridges lay over the crouching cavalrymen.

The screaming Kiowa outnumbered the small patrol five to one, but the deadly firepower of the Spencers kept the howling warriors at bay. The first few attacks were frontal charges, and charge after charge was broken before the Kiowa warhorses drew within fifty feet of the ensconced soldiers.

Then the bronzed warriors switched tactics, racing back and forth parallel to the ridges behind which the patrol crouched, firing from under their pony's neck as they swept past.

Sergeant Kincaid had shoved Emmeline Terry to the ground beside him where she buried her head in the side of the ridge, her hands pressed to her ears.

"Pick your targets, boys!" Lieutenant Tanner shouted, squinting through the smoke and levering another cartridge in his Spencer. He lined up the front sights on a screaming warrior leaning over the neck of his war pony and squeezed off a shot. The warrior jerked back and threw up his arms as he tumbled off the back of his horse.

Even before the warrior hit the ground, Tanner levered in another cartridge. The warriors reined their ponies around and retreated beyond range of the Spencers. "Load up, men!" he shouted. "They're bunching for another charge!"

"Come on, you red heathens! I got seven more slugs for you! You can join your brothers in the Happy Hunting Ground," Crocker shouted, referring to the eight warriors lying on the battlefield.

The warriors milled about, shouting, waving their

rifles over their heads, building their courage. They wheeled and made a wide circle to the south. As they drew near the caprock, a war cry galvanized them into action. Their ponies leaped forward. Each warrior hooked his foot in the saddle and leaned over the off side of his galloping pony so he could fire from under the horse's neck as he raced past the crouching cavalrymen.

The thunder of racing hooves rumbled through the air, and twelve screaming Kiowa charged.

"Here they come! Pick your target! Hold on, hold on!" Tanner shouted. "Now!"

The Spencers roared. Smoke billowed from the muzzles, and through the thickening smoke came the whinnies of injured ponies and the startled shouts of wounded warriors.

Zeke Tanner lined up his sights on the back of a retreating warrior. Taking his time, he squeezed the trigger, but as he did, he slid the front sight onto the breast of Private Cutch Barstow and fired.

The impact knocked Barstow to the ground where he struggled to sit up. Clutching at the spreading stain on his chest, he stared at Tanner, stunned, unable to believe his eyes. The lieutenant had shot him, deliberately. He opened his lips to speak out, but the words never came. He died within seconds.

"Keep firing, men!" Tanner shouted, turning his Spencer toward the retreating Kiowa.

Having had enough of the .50 Spencers, the Kiowa kept riding.

And the only time Tanner wasted in moving out after hastily burying Private Cutch Barstow was to throw Barstow's saddlebags on his horse.

Sergeant Kincaid stared at the dead Kiowa beyond the caprock. "Blasted heathens. All of you ain't worth old Cutch."

Tanner nodded. His face solemn, he said, "He was a good soldier. He died a hero. I'll recommend him for a medal."

Chapter Nine

The growing darkness was spreading over the woodland of thin grass, stunted oak, and tough mesquite when Josh and Leeboy rode into Zeke Tanner's old camp.

"Reckon we're closing the gap," Leeboy drawled.

Josh nodded. "Tomorrow's the day." He looked longingly to the north. "Sure would like to keep going." He peered at the ground, but it was too dark to make out any sign.

Leeboy swung down from the saddle and stomped his feet. "Yep, but we're best off giving our horses some rest and getting some ourselves. We're going to need all the strength we can muster when we catch up with Zeke."

While Josh picketed their horses, Leeboy laid a

small fire in the coals from the previous night and boiled some coffee. "You got your choice of meals— Army hardtack or Army jerky?"

"Reckon I'll have the jerky." Josh chuckled and rolled out his bedroll. "Last hardtack I ate looked like it had been paid a visit by worms."

Later, the fire burning low, each man lay between his blankets, staring at the starry heavens, lost in his own thoughts. The only sounds were the chirruping of crickets and the occasional cry of night birds.

Finally Leeboy broke the silence. "You reckon they hurt the girl?"

Josh mulled the question. "I don't know what's gone wrong with Zeke. He might have turned owlhoot or Copperhead, but I can't believed he'd do hurt to a woman."

Leeboy remained silent.

"Don't you think so?"

Releasing a breath of pent up air, Leeboy mumbled, "Yeah. I reckon." He muttered a soft curse. "But if last week someone had told me we'd be chasing Zeke Tanner like this, I'd have laughed in his face."

Josh knew the feeling.

Next morning while it was still dark, Josh looked around from where he was squatting before the fire. He shook his head as he watched his partner deliberately roll out on the right side of his bedroll. "You reckon your hair'd fall out if you got up on the left side of your blankets?"

"Laugh all you want." Leeboy snorted. "I ain't taking no chances on bad luck today. Getting out of bed on the right side will guarantee us good luck."

Grinning wryly, Josh turned back to the fire. In all the years he'd been partnering with Leeboy, he had not once seen the red-headed wrangler get out of bed on the left side.

By the time the sun rose, the two cowpokes had rolled their bedrolls, packed their gear, and were ready to ride. A few thin tendrils of smoke drifted from the dirt they had kicked over the fire.

Leeboy eased his pony to the north side of the clearing and studied the ground. "Here it is, Josh. Still heading north."

The lanky cowpoke pulled up beside his red-headed partner. "What are you waiting for? Let's go."

They moved out at a lope, eyes fixed on the hard ground. Several times within the first half-mile, the sign disappeared only to reappear a short distance farther. Finally they hit a stretch of softer ground. Instantly, each reined up, staring at the sign, puzzled.

"Something's wrong." Josh looked at Leeboy who was skirting around the sign on the ground.

Slowly, Leeboy shook his head, the freckles bunched

in patches on his freckled face. "Yep. Looks like eight horses." The frown on his face deepened. "That don't make sense. We followed eleven horses to the camp back yonder. Now we got eight."

For a moment, the two cowpokes stared at each other, then Josh's gaze slid back to the camp behind them. "Best we ride back and try to figure out what took place. Zeke's sly enough to try to out-slick us."

They studied the perimeter of the camp carefully, but the only sign leaving the camp headed north. "Reckon we need to do a little casting, huh?" Without waiting for an answer, Leeboy rode a few feet beyond the camp and started making a large circle. Josh rode in the opposite direction.

They met on the far side of the camp without cutting sign. Leeboy lifted an eyebrow. Josh shrugged. "We make a larger circle."

After two more unsuccessful efforts, Leeboy struck pay dirt. "Over here, Josh. Over here."

Josh grinned wryly when he spotted the three sets of tracks, one deeper than the other. "The gold."

"Reckon so." Leeboy looked eastward. "What do you suppose Zeke's got in mind? You'd think with hostiles about, he'd keep the gold with him. Why put it all on one horse now?"

This last move by Zeke puzzled Josh. Slowly he shook his head. "I got no idea, but we got no choice. We have to follow the gold."

"You reckon Zeke is with the gold?"

"I would be."

The sun beamed down, baking Josh's shoulders. He sipped from his canteen and offered it to Leeboy.

Studying the trail they were following, Leeboy sat saying, "Whoever is up there is pushing his horses mighty hard." He peered eastward. As far as the eye could see was a woodland of sun-blistered grass, stunted oak, and wiry mesquite.

Leeboy tilted his Stetson to the back of his head and dragged at the sweat on his forehead with the back of his arm. "It's so hot, I reckon prunes could stew in their own juice."

Josh grunted. "It'll get hotter."

And it did.

Just before dusk, Leeboy reined up abruptly and threw out his arm to halt Josh. "Over there. Straight ahead of us. That ain't a deer, is it?"

Josh squinted through the oak and mesquite. He grimaced. "That's no deer. It's an Indian. Too far to tell what kind, but I'd guess Comanche."

Leeboy muttered a soft curse as he moved his pony behind an oak. "What do you reckon is going on?"

"No idea," Josh muttered, glancing around for concealment, no matter how sparse. "Last thing we need is a bunch of Comanche coming down our throats." He spied a small copse of half a dozen stunted oak. "Over there. Maybe we can hide until he's gone."

Ten minutes later, both cowboys cursed, looking on in frustration while a band of forty or more warriors made camp where Leeboy had spotted the first one.

"Must've been their scout," he muttered, shaking his head. He looked around at Josh. "Now what?"

With a rueful chuckle, Josh said, "Now we wait." They dismounted and tied their horses to the trunk of one of the stunted oaks.

"We wait until they're asleep, and then we try to go around." He glanced at Leeboy's pocket in which he kept his lucky gold eagle. "You might rub your charm for us a couple of times."

Leeboy grinned. "I will."

Two hours after midnight, they moved out. In the distance, several fires in the Indian camp dotted the darkness. "I say we go north," Leeboy muttered. "The wind's from the south. I figure we can ride our ponies north, then when we cut east, we'll lead them. We'll have to pinch their nostrils to keep them from whinnying when they smell the Indian horses."

"We're going to have to walk a right good piece."

"Yep, but what do you want, that or forty or fifty angry Comanche chasing us?"

Josh chuckled. "Lead on. I'll follow."

There was no moon, but starlight filtered through the thin canopy of leaves overhead. They rode north thirty minutes, then turned east and dismounted. "Go ahead," Josh said. "I'll follow, but be careful where you step. Reckon this is a good night for snakes to hunt."

Leeboy groaned. "You coulda gone all day and not said that."

For an hour they walked east. "Reckon we can ride again?" Leeboy whispered over his shoulder. "These boots are hurting my feet something fierce."

Before Josh could answer, a shadowy figure rose from the ground in front of them.

"What the—" Leeboy said.

The figure threw up his arms and dropped to his knees. "Don't shoot, mister, please, don't shoot."

Josh tried to peer into the shadows in front of him, but Leeboy's horse was in his way. "What's going on?"

"I don't know," Leeboy whispered harshly. "A Mexican. Looks like a boy."

"Mexican? What's he doing out here?" He stopped beside Leeboy, squinting at the kneeling figure on the ground.

"Help me, *por favor.* I escape *el indio de Comanche.* For more than a year, I am prisoner. They kill me if they catch me. You must help, *en el nombre de Dios.*"

Leeboy looked around at Josh who growled impatiently, "As if we didn't have enough problems. Now we got us a child to bother with."

"We can't leave him out here."

"Blast it. Don't you think I know that?" He released a long sigh. "It just seems like everything is working against us."

Despite the shadows cast by the overhead leaves,

each saw the frustration on the other's face. "What else do you reckon can go wrong?" Leeboy muttered.

"I don't know, but I'll give you odds it will." Josh swung into his saddle and stared at the thin figure wearing a deerskin shirt and loincloth. He glanced at Leeboy. "You like youngsters so much, he can ride with you."

The red-headed cowpoke extended his arm to the kneeling youth. "Might as well come on, boy. We got a heap of riding to do, and I got the feeling when it's over, you'll wish you were back with the Comanche."

Josh grunted. "Amen to that."

After a few minutes, Josh spoke up. "I don't reckon getting out of bed this morning on the right side brought you much good luck, seeing as how we run into all those Comanche back there."

"Sure it did, partner. The Comanche didn't see us, did they?"

Josh just shook his head. Some jaspers were so knot-headed, you just couldn't argue with them.

Chapter Ten

Josh glanced back over his shoulder every few minutes as they kept their ponies in a walk, unwilling to chance the noise generated by trotting or loping their horses. After an hour, they kicked their animals into a gentle lope. After another hour, Josh reined up. "Let's take a breather. I'll keep watch while you and the boy grab forty winks. Then you can spell me. I want to be in the saddle when the sun comes."

"I ain't arguing with you on that," drawled Leeboy, dismounting and loosening the cinch. He glanced at the Mexican boy who was staring at them silently. He appeared to be around twelve or thirteen. "What do they call you, boy?"

His white teeth stood out in the shadows when he

grinned. "They call me, Luis, *senor*. My papa, he name me Luis Alvarado Elizio Guadalupe Martinez."

Josh lifted an eyebrow as he listened to the conversation while rolling out his blankets.

Leeboy chuckled. "That's a mighty heavy handle for such a little boy, Luis."

With a touch of bravado in his thin voice, Luis replied, "But I am strong, *senor*. That is why I remained alive. The Comanche, they like strong boys."

Rolling out his own soogan, Leeboy asked, "Where's your family?"

Luis shook his head slowly and dropped his chin to his chest. "Dead. The Comanche, they kill Papa and Mamacita when they raided our farm and steal me."

Leeboy sat on his blankets and fumbled through his saddlebags. "Here," he said, tossing a strip of jerky to the boy, "chew on this."

"And you can roll up in this," Josh added gruffly, tossing the youth a blanket. Leeboy looked up. Josh shrugged when he saw the amusement on his partner's face. "Well, the boy can't sleep on the ground."

Leeboy shook Josh awake. "Time. Sun'll be up in a few minutes."

At the same time Josh and Leeboy rode out, Zeke Tanner broke camp a hundred miles to the northwest. He headed directly north behind Gian-nah-tah, and throughout the day, the distance between the two groups continued to grow.

Sergeant Kincaid rode up beside Tanner and glanced at Emmeline Terry who slumped wearily in her saddle. "She's about wore out, Lieutenant."

Tanner took a quick look. The young woman rode with her chin on her chest, eyes closed, her thin body rocking in the saddle with each step of her bay.

Kincaid waited for a response. When it didn't come, he spoke more emphatically. "She ain't never going to make it to La Junta."

Zeke Tanner shot Kincaid a fiery glance. "When I want your opinion, Sergeant, I'll ask for it."

Kincaid bristled. For a moment, he stared Tanner in the eyes. "Yes, sir," he replied, clenching his teeth. "Just thought you might like to know. Sorry to have bothered you, Lieutenant, sir." He wheeled around and galloped to the rear of the column, preferring to eat dust than be in the proximity of Lieutenant Tanner.

Keeping his eyes forward, Tanner knew Kincaid was right, but what Kincaid didn't know was the patrol would never reach La Junta. In two days, they would make Palo Duro Canyon, and Emmeline Terry could make it that far.

After breaking camp, Leeboy and Josh headed south, planning to ride thirty minutes, the same length of time they had ridden north earlier that morning. Twenty minutes later, Josh's pony stiffened and perked his ears forward. Josh reined up, squinting in the direction his horse was looking. "Look yonder. That tree line. Looks like a creek."

"Out here?"

"Won't hurt to see."

The creek was dry, but in the middle of the sandy bed were three sets of tracks, one deeper than the others. The two cowboys grinned at each other. Leeboy patted his lucky gold eagle and with smug satisfaction said, "Reckon it's still working."

Josh chuckled. "Reckon so."

Luis frowned at the enigmatic exchange of words.

A hundred yards to the east, the trail left the creek bed and angled northeast. Mile after mile, they rode through an unchanging woodland of sun-parched grass, stunted oak, and mesquite. The thin canopy of leaves did little to dispel the intensity of the August sun.

Josh felt as limp as a worn-out rope, but stubbornly he stayed on the trail. Leeboy was no better off, and Luis rode with his chin on his chest. Heads drooping, the horses trudged wearily, kicking up puffs of dust with their hooves. The debilitating heat drained the energy and strength from both man and beast.

Just before dusk, Josh's bay looked up, suddenly alert. His abrupt movement snapped Josh out of the lethargy induced by the heat and the rhythmic gait of his pony. "What is it, boy?" He squinted into the fading light. A light-colored object lay on the ground a few hundred yards distant.

"What?" Leeboy asked.

Josh dipped his head, gesturing ahead of them. "In

front of us. Can you make it out?" He eased his sidearm from the holster.

"Not from here. Let's take a look."

Slowly, they rode forward, guns drawn. Luis peered around Leeboy, curious as to what had caught the attention of the two men.

Suddenly, Leeboy said, "Ain't that the horse with the gold?"

"Sure looks like it." Josh frowned and quickly searched the countryside around them, wondering just where Tanner and his man were. He saw nothing.

"Something don't feel right, Josh. Do it to you?"

"Reckon not. Just keep your eyes moving until we find out what the Sam Hill is going on here." They rode on.

"Sure looks dead to me, and it looks like the gold is still in the packsaddles."

Josh scanned the terrain around them. Still nothing. An uneasy feeling began nagging at him. "No way they'd leave the gold out here all by its lonesome."

They reined up and exchanged puzzled looks.

"Comanche?"

"No." He nodded to the area around them. "No sign."

"Look, it ain't dead," said Leeboy. "It's still breathing."

Legs extended, the dapple-gray lay on his side, its breath coming in shallow, rasping gasps. Josh frowned.

Something was wrong. Something was very wrong. The uneasiness that had settled on his shoulders when he first spotted the downed horse grew more intense.

"Keep your eyes moving," Josh said, quickly dismounting and slashing open the canvas packsaddle. White rocks poured out.

Stunned, the lanky cowpoke gaped at the pile of rocks. He looked up at Leeboy in disbelief. He squeezed his eyes shut and, cursing at the top of his lungs, jammed his revolver back in its holster. "That blasted Zeke Tanner. He snookered us. For two days, he snookered us, that no-good—" His tirade ended in a sputtering of words.

Leeboy cut him off. "Stop yammering and mount up. We got us some riding to do."

Josh caught his breath. "You cut their trail. They can't be far ahead." He pulled out his knife and slashed the packsaddle from the wheezing horse. He rose to his feet and stared down at the exhausted animal. "I reckon I ought to put you out of your misery, old boy." He reached for his sixgun, but as he did, the dapple-gray snorted and struggled to its feet where it stood uncertainly.

Josh hesitated, then holstered his handgun, slipped the bridle from the gray, and gave it a slap on its rump. He swung into the saddle. Leeboy was grinning at him. Gruffly, Josh remarked, "Well, he's on his feet. He can take care of himself. Now, what about their trail?"

The red-headed cowpoke pointed northwest. "Like the crow flies. One shod, one unshod. That sneaky Zeke

Tanner sent us on a two-day wild goose chase while he gets farther and farther away."

"Don't worry," Josh said, following the trail at a lope. "We'll catch up with him."

The two sets of tracks were fresh, easy to follow at a mile-eating lope. Within thirty minutes, the tracks were lost in the fading light, but knowing they would cut Tanner's trail sooner or later, the two cowboys continued northwest well into the starlit night. Around midnight, Leeboy's horse stumbled, almost spilling him and Luis, which was reason enough to pull up and give their ponies a rest.

Throughout the day, the young Mexican had bounced up and down on the rump of Leeboy's horse without uttering a word of complaint or discomfort. Despite Josh's impatience with children, he couldn't help admiring the boy's grit. Probably got it from the Comanche, he told himself.

Well before the sun rose, they were riding hard. This time Josh carried the young boy to give Leeboy's pony a rest.

They rode hard for an hour, then easy for an hour. Dust stung their eyes, caked their faces. Just before noon, they ran across a small creek rising from a jumble of limestone boulders and flowing generally southeast.

The water was cold and sweet, refreshing the weary men and boy, giving them strength to face an interminable afternoon under the blistering sun.

Leeboy swung back into the saddle. "What if we can't find the trail?"

Josh hooked his thumb to the south. "Then we go back as far as we have to and pick it up." He adjusted the cinch on his saddle and squinted toward the building clouds to the north. "But, we'll find it."

His prediction came true in mid-afternoon when they cut a trail heading north. "I count eight or nine sets. How about you?"

Leeboy rode down the backtrail, studying the sign. "I make out eight, but I don't see any evidence of the gold. All of the tracks except one set are about the same depth."

"Umm, yep, see what you mean." Josh lifted his gaze from the ground and stared at Leeboy. "That odd set must be the girl."

"What about the gold?"

Josh glanced northward. He couldn't resist an admiring grin for Zeke's sly trick. "Think about it a minute. What would you do to keep from leaving a set of tracks deeper than the others?"

Leeboy frowned, considering the question. The frown suddenly faded into a grin. "Why, that sneaky . . . yeah, I'd do the same thing. I'd spread the gold around so all the tracks looked the same—that none cut deeper than the others."

"That Zeke, he's a tricky one." He nudged his heels in his bay's flank. "Let's get after them."

Three hours later, they ran across the site of Tanner's fight with the Kiowa. Several Indian ponies and a single cavalry remount lay dead. "Looks like they hid back in the ridges on the slope," Josh said, studying the empty cartridge shells strewn about. He shifted his gaze to the top of the slope, then let it slide northward along the rim, recognizing the fact a whole passel of Comanche or Kiowa could be standing less than twenty feet from the rim high above and still be out of his sight. Josh reminded himself to keep a wary eye on the caprock as they continued their pursuit of Zeke Tanner.

"There's one of them that ain't going to have no more breakfasts," Leeboy said, pointing to a grave covered with fair-sized rocks.

The two old friends looked at each other, each asking himself the same question. "Zeke?" asked Leeboy.

Josh cleared his throat. "I doubt it, but we best make sure." He glanced over his shoulder. "Keep one eye open. Some of those Kiowa might still be around."

Leeboy shuddered. "Bad luck to dig up the dead."

"Maybe so, but it's worse luck not to know the strength of your enemy," he replied, climbing off his horse and removing the rocks from the head of the grave.

A foot down, they found a blue coat. Josh looked up at Leeboy. "Well, at least now we know Zeke ain't no outlaw."

Leeboy's lips curled in anger. "Just as bad. He's a Copperhead."

Josh bent back over. "Let's see if this is him."

Both men gave a sigh of relief when the swollen face beneath the coat was not that of Zeke Tanner.

After swinging back into the saddle and picking up the trail again, both cowboys remained silent for several long minutes, each lost in his own thoughts. Finally Leeboy broke the silence. "What do you think made Zeke turn Copperhead?"

Pondering the question, Josh shook his head slowly. "No idea. Of course, you know Zeke always had some ornery ways. More than once before he was killed, my pa would grab me by the scruff of my neck and swear he would blister me good if I ever did some of the things Zeke had done. Seems like Zeke was always looking for trouble, and when he wasn't, trouble up and found him."

Leeboy grunted. "Yep, like we said the other day, seems like Zeke always had the notion folks was out to take advantage of him."

"But why would that make him turn Copperhead? What little I had to do with Yankees, I didn't find them much different than us except they talk funny."

"Don't reckon I got an answer for that."

"Maybe the answer is nothing more than the fact people change."

Josh lifted an eyebrow. "Could be that's just as good an answer as there is. Maybe the only answer in his case." He nodded to the pocket in which Leeboy carried the gold eagle. "You think that good luck charm of yours there is what made you smart enough to come up with that answer?"

Leeboy glared at his partner. His eyes narrowed when he realized Josh was teasing. "Go to blazes!"

Chapter Eleven

That night Lieutenant Tanner made camp on the edge of the thinly forested country through which they had been traveling. To the north lay an arid tableland dotted with mesquite, a sprinkling of juniper, and cotton-woods and willow along the streambeds.

Knowing they would reach Palo Duro Canyon the next day, he decided to make camp early, forgoing the nightly routine of traveling until midnight.

Later that night after a sparse meal of Confederate hardtack and thick coffee, Tanner sat near the edge of the firelight studying his small party.

Sergeant Kincaid, as always, kept to himself. Private Serra and Corporal Crocker sat on their blankets playing poker, not for money, which Tanner had forbidden, but to pass the time. The youngest, Luther Webb, had fallen into the sleep of the innocent. Tanner grimaced as he studied the slumbering youth. He would be the last and hardest to kill because Zeke truly liked the young man. The others, he could execute without compunction.

A cough from the darkness beyond the firelight arrested his attention. He glanced into the night, knowing Gian-nah-tah and Black Fox lay out there, their black eyes watching the camp. Those two would prove to be the most difficult to kill.

He turned up his tin cup and sipped the last of his coffee, spitting out the grounds that had flowed onto his tongue. His wary eyes shifted to the frail form of Emmeline Terry, her pale face smudged with dust, her blond hair tangled, sleeping fitfully.

Tanner had not decided what to do with her. All he knew for certain was he could not kill a woman, nor sell her to the Comanches.

The next day just before noon, Gian-nah-tah held up his hand and reined his warhorse to a halt. Tanner pulled up beside him. "What do you see?"

Pointing to a ridge layered with red claystone and white gypsum rising three hundred feet above the prairie, the Apache replied, "Canyon of Hard Wood." At the base of the ridge was a line of green marking the river. Above the ridge, billowing white clouds drifted across a sky of robin's-egg blue.

While the caprock continued northward to the thicket along the North Canadian River, Palo Duro Canyon cut back to the northwest, its rugged slopes overlooking a floor of undulating hills rounded by millenniums of weather, sharp pinnacles piercing the sky, oblong mesas, and the smaller buttes. Along with tough hackberries, wiry juniper and stunted mesquite struggled to grow in the harsh conditions of the canyon.

While Tanner had never approached Palo Duro from the south, he was familiar with the mouth of the canyon, having spent almost a year wandering the length of the one hundred and twenty mile canyon, which in places was almost twenty miles wide and eight-hundred-feet deep.

Though it had not the breathtaking magnificence of the great canyon he had seen in northern Arizona Territory, the one the Paiutes called Kaibab or 'Mountain Lying Down,' Palo Duro possessed its own awe-inspiring grandeur.

As they drew closer to the canyon, Tanner rode up beside Gian-nah-tah. "Two hours up the canyon, a small stream empties into the river. Do you know of it?"

The Apache nodded. "I know. The Fork of the Snake."

"That is where we will camp tonight."

His thin lips compressed, Gian-nah-tah nodded, saying no more.

Zeke Tanner knew the campsite well. He had deliberately selected it when he first made his plan to steal the Confederate gold. There was water and shelter, and the location was far enough from the Comanche rancherias at the furthermost upper reaches of the great canyon that he should have no contact with them. He figured he could remain encamped there until any pursuit had given up.

The afternoon sun baked the countryside mercilessly. Leaves wilted from a searing heat that sucked the breath away. "Take a look, Josh," said Leeboy, his sweat-soaked shirt clinging to his thin frame.

Directly in front of them, two sets of tracks, one shod, the other unshod, joined those they had been following. "Looks like our friends hooked up with Tanner, don't it?"

Leeboy studied the tracks, noting how the bent grass was straightening itself. "Yep. Hard to say how old they are, but I figure they were made sometime today."

"Looks that way." Josh removed his Stetson and wiped his face with his neckerchief, studying the caprock off to his left. "One thing for certain, Zeke's changed his tactics. His trail hasn't strayed one way or another from due north."

Leeboy looked around at Luis. "How you doing, boy?"

The young boy nodded. "*Hago bien*. I do well."

Winking at Josh, Leeboy teased the young boy. "You ain't tired some?"

Luis straightened his shoulders. "*Yo no me canso*. I do not grow tired."

Touching his heels to his bay, Josh grunted. "You're a better man than me then. Hold on. We're moving out."

As they loped along the trail, Leeboy squinted to the north. "I wouldn't swear for sure, Josh, but I think we're heading to that big canyon we ran across years ago when we drifted down this way from Denver. You think? What was it's name, Palo Duro?"

"Something like that," he replied looking around for landmarks in the woodland through which they rode. "I'm not right certain just where we are, but that canyon is around here somewhere, I reckon."

Thirty minutes later, they spotted the first of the juniper, a small evergreen shrub with needlelike foliage, the skeletal branches of which grabbed at the air like witches' fingers.

The country into which they rode grew arid, the ground baked hard by the unrelenting sun, the air thinner and drier.

Josh studied the trail before them. The tracks were closer together, indicating a growing weariness in the horses. "Best I can tell, we're probably a couple hours back. We ought to spot their camp tonight."

"Maybe we should find us a spot to hole up, then ride on in after dark."

"Lets us get a little closer." He squinted into the distance. "Look out there, on the horizon. Isn't that a break in the caprock?"

Leeboy stood in his stirrups and tugged his hat brim down on his forehead to shade his eyes. Excited, he replied, "You dadgummed tootin' it is. That's Palo Duro."

Thirty minutes later, they spotted a line of green along the base of a multihued ridge made up of layers of red, yellow, white, and lavender. "There's the river," Leeboy announced. He glanced at the sun. "Wonder if it's dry?"

"The way our luck has been running, it's probably drier than an empty water barrel."

To their relief, a thin stream wound its way down the distant side of the sandy bed. The far shore beneath the steep caprock was lined with feathery willow trees and ancient cottonwoods, their green crowns blanketing the ground below with cool, welcome shade.

"Looks like they headed up into the canyon," said Leeboy, pointing to the trail.

Josh studied the canyon several seconds. "No telling where they are up there. They could be half-a-mile, or they could be ten miles. As I remember this place, it's full of canyons that could hide an entire battalion of cavalry." He looked around at Leeboy. "They could be watching us right now."

A devil-may-care grin played over Leeboy's lips. "Well, if they are, we can't do nothing it about now." He nodded to the inviting shade across the river. "If they're watching, then they can watch me mosey over there and take off my boots and splash my feet in the water."

* * *

Ten minutes later, they had dismounted in the shade of the cottonwoods and loosened the cinches on their saddles. The breeze wafting along the base of the ridge blew through their sweat-dampened shirts, cooling them pleasantly.

Leeboy plopped to the ground and promptly removed his gunbelt and boots. His socks in his hand, he motioned to Luis. "Come on, boy. Lets take us a bath. Coming Josh?"

"You two go ahead," he said. "I'll keep watch."

"Well, then, just make sure you stay downwind of Luis and me, you hear? I hated to mention it earlier, but you're getting kinda rank."

The young Mexican boy promptly lay down in the shallow water. Leeboy grinned and peeled off his plaid shirt. He stuck it in the water, then slipped it back on. "Ahh. That does feel cool. You don't know what you're missing, Josh."

Josh just grinned and watched as his partner washed his socks and tossed them on the shore. He turned his eyes back into the canyon, searching the blue sky for telltale smoke in an effort to pinpoint Zeke's camp.

He studied the steep slope above him. He guessed it to be two or three hundred feet high. He wondered how old it was, how long it had taken the lazy river to carve it out. As he studied the precipitous ridges up and down the river, his gaze caught what appeared to be a crevice a hundred yards or so upriver. Curious, he picked his way through the tumble of rock and debris toward it.

"Hey! Where you going?"

Josh glanced back and shook his head, pointing to the crevice. "See what that is."

Leeboy shrugged and kicked water at Luis playfully.

To Josh's surprise, the crevice was about four feet wide, and the entrance was worn smooth, an indication someone at some point had come and gone many times. He stepped into its shadows, taking care to search the floor ahead for the deadly diamondback rattlesnakes that populated Palo Duro.

After a few feet, the passageway turned sharply. He halted, peering into the darkness beyond. He could see nothing, but he had the distinct feeling the passage opened into a large room.

Chapter Twelve

At the Fork of the Snake, Tanner led the patrol across the river, which, though shallow, was over a hundred feet wide. On the north side of the river, he urged his horse through a copse of cottonwood behind which was the mouth of a branch canyon. He reined up at a tiny spring flowing from the lavender-colored mudstone at the base of a cliff that rose several feet to an overhang of white gypsum.

Emmeline Terry looked around anxiously, but Tanner ignored her. "We camp here."

Sergeant Kincaid frowned as he studied the layout. "What about our horses, Lieutenant?"

Tanner grinned and nodded to a gap in the face of the caprock. "That opening leads to a natural corral with water and graze. The only way the animals can be spotted is from the caprock above."

"So, what's your plan, Lieutenant?"

Zeke gestured to their surroundings. "We rest up here a couple of days. I'm sending Gian-nah-tah and Black Fox ahead to scout for hostiles. If it looks clear, we'll bail out for La Junta."

Kincaid grinned and nodded. "Yes, sir."

"All right, Sergeant. Put the men to making camp. Tell Luther to look after the woman."

The sergeant touched his fingers to the brim of his Hardy hat in a sloppy salute, then barked orders to the men.

While the men bustled about, Tanner made his way downriver, ostensibly to scout the terrain, but in truth to make certain the cave with the bottomless pit had not caved in.

With the two savages out of the camp, he could begin to carry out the rest of his plan. Kincaid would be the first. He was the most dangerous. He would go in the pit. The remaining cavalrymen were of no danger to him. He'd simply shoot them while they were out scouting for the vanished Sergeant Kincaid. The birds and varmints of Palo Duro would make quick work of their carcasses.

When Leeboy and Luis waded from the river, they found Josh building a torch. "What's going on, partner?"

"A cave. Looks like it's seen a heap of use. We might have found us a temporary boardinghouse."

"Hold on. I'll go with you."

"Best you keep an eye peeled out here." He nodded to the cave. "Wouldn't do for us to get ourselves trapped in there."

Leeboy shrugged and laid his hand on Luis' shoulder. "Well, then, boy. Let's you and me chew on some hardtack and keep our eyes peeled. Okey-dokey?"

With a bright grin on his dark face, Luis nodded and patted his stomach. "Okey-dokey."

With a torch in one hand and a thick, dead branch in the other as a precaution in case of a run-in with a diamondback, Josh entered the cave. Turning the first corner, he saw he had been right. The narrow passage opened into a large room. In the middle was a scattering of ashes, spread by scurrying rodents and slithering snakes.

He held the torch closer, seeing three or four serpentine trails. Tightening his grip on the torch, he held it at arm's length. The room appeared to be thirty or so feet square with a ceiling beyond the height of the dancing light cast by the torch.

Along one wall were several piles of horse biscuits, dried to powder. On the opposite wall was another passage, which, he discovered, led into an even larger chamber. "Looks like we found us a home, at least for the night," he mumbled, heading back up the passage to the first chamber.

As Josh stepped into the open room, something hit the brim of his Stetson. He leaped forward, then spun and thrust the torch at the passage from which he had just emerged. The terrifying hum of rattles echoed through the chamber. Sudden fear pumped adrenaline through his veins. His heart raced.

Coiled on a ledge several feet above the cave floor was an angry diamondback, its head poised for another strike. Josh swung the dead branch at the buzzing rattlesnake, knocking it to the floor. The thick-bodied serpent hit the floor and instantly coiled its wiry body, but before it managed another strike, Josh crushed its head.

Quickly, he held the torch above his head, searching the walls for any other rattlers. With a sigh of relief, he spotted none. Glancing back at the dead snake, he muttered, "At least, we'll have something different for supper than hardtack."

Within an hour, a fire blazed in the first chamber with chunks of rattlesnake sizzling on spits. While Josh and Leeboy picketed the horses next to one wall and gathered what graze they could, Luis disappeared into the second chamber.

When they finished tending the horses, Josh noticed the young boy was missing. A puzzled frown wrinkled his forehead. "Where's the boy?"

Leeboy glanced around. "No idea."

At that moment, the glow of a torch shone from the second chamber and Luis appeared, holding a headless diamondback by the rattles. He pointed his knife at the sizzling meat at the fire and extended his arm with the rattler in their direction. "Now, we have much to eat."

For a moment, Josh was speechless, then he cautioned the youth. "Those critters can hurt you bad, boy."

Luis grinned up at Josh and held the rattlesnake higher. "I catch many. Not bite Luis."

Josh lifted a skeptical eyebrow. "Don't go and get too confident on us now, boy."

Zeke Tanner cursed as he stared at the boulders and detritus filling the mouth of the cave. He shook his head and grunted. "Reckon you'll have to take a bullet just like the others, Sergeant," he muttered.

"All the comforts of home," Leeboy drawled, sipping sixshooter coffee and filling his belly with broiled rattlesnake. He glanced around the chamber. "A jasper could set up living in a place like this. Water right outside the door, place for the horses, even a spare room for guests." He laughed and nodded to the adjoining chamber.

"As long as you don't mind uninvited guests," Josh replied, popping a chunk of snake in his mouth and pushing himself to his feet. He crossed the room and peered around the corner of the passage. "It's good and dark outside," he announced, turning back to Leeboy and Luis. "I reckon it's about time to head out."

Luis jumped to his feet, but Josh stayed him. "You stay. No telling what we might run into out there."

"I am not a rabbit. I am not afraid."

Leeboy chuckled. "We know, Luis. What Josh is trying to say is that there could be shooting. You could pick up a stray bullet." He shook his head. "It's best you stay. Look after things here for us."

There was no moon, but the canyon was lit by the bluish-silver light of the glittering stars. A breeze had sprung up, bringing with it a hint of possible change in the weather.

Leeboy's eyes searched the shadows around him. "I reckon this is sort of like the blind leading the blind, huh?"

Josh chuckled. "Reckon so. Probably our best chance of stumbling across them is to make our way up the side of the caprock yonder until we can get a good view of the canyon. With a little luck, we might spot their campfire."

Leeboy patted his pocket. "I got my good luck piece with me, so don't worry, partner. We'll find them."

Thirty minutes later, they reined up, two hundred feet above the canyon floor on a rugged slope leading to the caprock another two hundred feet above. Spread before them, the rounded ridges of the canyon floor lay in stark relief in the starlight, patches of silver-blue interspersed with strips of blackness. In the distance, jagged pinnacle rose over sprawling mesas and buttes.

"I don't see nothing."

"Me neither," replied Josh. "Guess that means we ride on a farther piece and try again." To the east, a waxing moon, in its first quarter, rose, lighting the canyon.

Several times over the next four hours, they climbed the steep slopes of the caprock, studied the canyon, and moved on. Josh glanced at the Big Dipper. "About five or so," he announced. "Sun'll be up shortly. Reckon it's time to head back. I guess our best bet is just to get back on the Zeke's trail and keep our eyes peeled."

Leeboy snorted in disgust and reined his pony around. "Sure is aggravating. Why—hey, look! To the northwest. Ain't that a fire?"

"Where?" Josh squinted into the darkness.

"Over there. See that large formation that looks like a church steeple? To the right. You have to look hard. It comes and goes."

Josh strained to penetrate the night. Suddenly, a yellow speck flickered, then vanished, then reappeared. "Now, I see it."

"Looks to me like it's over by the river. It's probably the wind blowing tree branches that makes it keep disappearing."

"Probably," Josh replied. "Well, lets us take a look."

"Sun'll be up soon."

"Then I reckon we'll have to find us a place to hole up during the day."

Leeboy cast a glance in the direction of the cave. "You think Luis'll be all right back there?"

Josh chuckled. "Any hombre, man or boy, who can catch diamondbacks doesn't have a thing to worry about. You want to worry about something, old friend," he added with a grim smile, "worry about us getting caught out here in daylight. Let's just hope we can find a spot on these ridges to fort up where we can keep an eye on Zeke."

As false dawn rolled across the canyon, the distant caprock on the north side rose from the gray shadows of night like a monolith materializing out of a thick fog. Using the church steeple formation as a guide, Josh tried to find out a landmark to pinpoint the location of the campfire. He knew the lay of the land appeared entirely different in the harsh light of day.

"There's the river," Leeboy pointed out from their refuge in a deep gully. "And the trees that kept blocking the fire last night."

"Yep. You see where the caprock cuts back north? Just about at that cluster of cottonwoods. The campfire was right in through there."

"You sure?"

Removing his Stetson, Josh ran his fingers through

his sandy hair. "I'm not sure of anything yet. What was it you said last night, the blind leading the blind?"

The grin on Leeboy's face froze, then exploded into excitement. "Josh! Over there, to the left of those cottonwoods. Ain't that smoke?"

Chapter Thirteen

With the coming of dawn, the wind died, and a thin tendril of white smoke drifted lazily into the blue sky.

"Has to be Zeke," Josh said.

"Even if it is, how are we going to get over there?" Leeboy nodded to the rolling terrain between their hideaway and the smoke. "There's a heap of open spaces out there. We'd be mighty easy to spot."

Josh pondered their predicament a moment. "I suppose we'll have to head back south a piece until we're out of sight, then cut over. If they do spot us, with luck they'll just figure we're two drifters heading south." He reined around. "Let's go."

Leeboy lifted an eyebrow and grinned mischievously. "What if that ain't them?"

"Then we've wasted a lot of time," he said, nudging

his bay in the flanks. "To be on the safe side, why don't you give that lucky coin of yours an extra rub or two?"

"Thought you didn't believe in those old wives' tales?"

After an hour of riding, they cut toward the river, planning on finding a secluded spot to fort up for the day before making their way up the north side of the river after dark. "We best water our ponies and fill our canteens," Leeboy said, reining up on the north shore and dismounting.

The day dragged. Finally, the blazing ball of fire in the sky dropped below the horizon, accompanied by lavenders and orange splashed across the western sky.

Five minutes later, Josh and Leeboy headed north, staying on the shore near the water. Throughout the day, Josh worried Zeke might move out, but reassured himself that even if his old friend did break camp, he couldn't hide the sign of nine ponies.

"We're going to have a moon tonight," Leeboy muttered. "We best do whatever is we're going to do fast before it comes up."

An hour later, they spotted the campfire. "There it is," whispered Josh. "Pull up." They sat on their horses in the shadows of the cottonwoods studying the distant flame.

Josh handed Leeboy his reins. "Here. I'm going ahead on foot. See what I can see." Leeboy started to protest, but Josh stopped him. "They get me, you high-tail it out of here. At least, you can tell the captain back at Chadbourne what took place."

His jaw clenched, Leeboy nodded. "Just don't stumble over those big feet of yours."

"Don't worry." Josh dismounted and in the next second, vanished into the darkness cast by the cottonwoods.

He darted from tree to tree, trying to remain on hard ground so as not to leave any sign for a wandering eye to spot, a task almost impossible at night. When he was within fifty yards or so of the camp, his toe caught a small boulder and with a grunt, he lurched into a cottonwood, scraping the side of his face on the rugged bark of the tree. He froze, straining for any indication someone had heard the noise and was coming to investigate.

After a few moments, satisfied his commotion had gone unnoticed, he crept forward.

The campfire flickered through a thick growth of cottonwoods, offering an ideal spot from which he could survey the camp. But, he reminded himself as he studied the dark copse of tall trees, Zeke could have posted a guard in those very shadows, a guard who would see Josh as soon as he stepped into the open.

For the next fifteen minutes, the lanky cowpoke peered around the trunk of a large cottonwood, his eyes searching every inch of the shadows cast by the cluster of trees.

Finally, having seen no movement, he took a deep breath and muttered, "Might as well kick open the door and see what's inside."

Like a wraith, he ghosted from tree to tree, and in a final burst of speed, dashed into the deep shadows of the motte of trees, pressing up against the rugged bark of a cottonwood and straining to listen for any threatening sounds.

There was nothing.

He peered around the trunk. The camp was fifty or so feet distant. He spotted Zeke immediately, then quickly counted four Union cavalrymen. He searched the camp for the young woman, momentarily alarmed at her absence. Then he sighted her sitting on her blankets, which were spread far from the others.

"Looks no worse for wear," Josh muttered under his breath. His eyes never stopped moving, searching now for the Indians. Two of them if he read the sign right. They were nowhere to be seen. He jerked around, squinting in an effort to penetrate the shadows around him, half expecting to see one or both savages leaping at him. But again, the night was silent except for the chirping of the night birds and the mournful wailing of coyotes.

Stealthily, he dropped into a crouch and eased forward until he could hear the brief conversation between Zeke and his sergeant.

"How much long you figure the two Injuns to be gone, Lieutenant?"

"Hard to say. They got over a hundred miles to cover, spotting any bands of Kiowa or Comanche. I'll give 'em a week before I figure they probably got themselves killed off."

The sergeant looked around. For a moment, Josh thought the bearded sergeant was staring directly at him. He remained motionless, every muscle frozen. Finally the sergeant turned back to Zeke. "So you plan on us staying here until they come back?"

Zeke studied Sergeant Kincaid several moments. Finally, he dismissed the sergeant with a single word. "Yes."

At that moment, the young woman rose and approached Tanner. She glared at him defiantly. "I'm going to the river and wash. If you have no objection," she added caustically.

With an indifferent shrug, Zeke nodded to the river.

"And make certain no one follows me," she snapped over her shoulder as she disappeared from the firelight, heading directly for Josh.

Serra and Crocker watched her with hungry eyes, but neither made a motion toward following. Josh grinned to himself. At least Zeke still maintained his respect for womanhood.

He pressed himself against the trunk of the cotton-wood as Emmeline walked along the trail, passing so close Josh could have reached out and touched her. He wanted to talk to her, but how?

If he grabbed her, she'd scream, and in less than ten seconds he'd have Union blueboys all over him like flies on a sore. Then, he had an idea.

Searching the ground at his feet, he found three or four small pebbles. Silently, he trailed after her, slipping from tree to tree until he was less than twenty feet from her. He glanced back at the camp, almost a hundred feet.

She knelt at the river's edge and dabbed a handkerchief into the cool water and patted her face and throat. Josh tossed a pebble over her head into the river. She stiffened at the splash. He tossed another one, this time a few feet downriver.

Emmeline jerked her head around at the splash. She looked back toward the camp.

Josh crossed his fingers, hoping she wouldn't scream. "Keep washing," he whispered. "I'm a friend. I'm here to help." For a moment, she remained motionless, undecided. "I buried your father and brother. Now, do what I say. Keep washing. We don't want them to think anything is going on."

For several seconds, the night air was tense with uncertainty, and then to his relief, she nodded and turned back to the river. In a soft whisper, she asked, "Who are you?"

"That isn't important. Now listen. We can't do anything right now, but tomorrow night, be ready to run."

"Where? When?"

"You'll know when. There's a thick cluster of cottonwoods fifty feet or so from the camp. You know where it is?"

"Yes."

"When the excitement starts, I'll meet you there."

"All right."

"Where are their horses? I didn't see any."

"In a natural corral behind the camp. The only way it can be seen is from above. At least, that's what the lieutenant said."

"All right. Don't leave the camp after dark tomorrow. When you make your break, go straight to the cottonwoods. Don't go down any of the trails."

Zeke Tanner's voice carried through the night. "You all right down there?"

Josh whispered, "Answer him, then go back. Remember tomorrow night."

"Yes. I'm perfectly all right," she called out, catching a glimpse of a shadow disappearing downriver.

Leeboy grinned when Josh told him they were going to steal the young woman the next night. "Fine with me, but do you have any idea how we're going to do it?"

"We can't match up with their firepower. But maybe we can stir up enough commotion to sway things in our favor."

"Commotion?" The red-headed cowpoke scratched his head. "How you going to do that?"

"Two ways. First, they keep their horses in a natural corral that can only be seen from above. What do you reckon those broomtails would do if a couple of burning balls of juniper came tumbling from the top of the cliff into their corral?"

Leeboy chuckled. "What's the second way?"

"Your friend, Luis."

"Luis?"

"And his snakes. Here's what I got in mind. I spotted three trails leading in and out of the camp. We'll stretch a line across each of the trails and dangle a diamondback across it, and then, we'll heave a bag of snakes into the camp. About that time, you kick the fire into the corral. When all the commotion starts, I'll get the girl. We'll meet downriver."

Leeboy stared at Josh for several seconds, the starlight showing the disbelief on his face. "You're crazy, you know it?"

Josh grinned.

"I've let you talk me into a heap of screwy notions like the time down in San Antone when we rode that bull up the stairs to the mezzanine of the Menger Hotel, but this is the dumbest I ever heard."

Josh's grin grew broader.

Leeboy narrowed his eyes. "You think I'm going to go along with you on this nutty idea, don't you?"

"Well, aren't you?"

With a disgusted snort, Leeboy growled, "Of course, but not because it's a good idea. Somebody's got to look after you."

Chapter Fourteen

Using blankets from their soogans, Josh and Leeboy fashioned bags for the snakes. Josh held one up. "Think this bag will hold the snakes, boy?"

Luis nodded. "Do good."

Josh and Leeboy exchanged concerned looks. Neither would admit it, but they were not looking forward to accompanying Luis into the depths of the cave searching for diamondbacks anymore than they would enjoy squatting on a cactus with their longjohns unbuttoned. "I'll follow behind Luis and hold the bags. You bring up the rear, with your hogleg in hand. You hear?"

Leeboy gulped. "I sure ain't taking any pleasure in this."

"You think I am?" Josh turned to Luis who was wearing a wide grin. "You ready?"

The young Mexican boy nodded enthusiastically. *"Si."* He held up a stiff branch six feet long with a double strand of woven deerskin running its length and forming a loop at the end. "We catch many *las serpientes* with this." He held it out and pulled on the leather cord. The loop snapped shut. He released one of the strands, and the loop opened.

Leeboy arched an eyebrow. "Slick. Just like a rabbit snare. You sure it works on snakes?"

Luis nodded again. *"Si.* This is how the Comanche catches *las serpientes."*

Taking a deep breath, Josh said, "Well, let's stop wasting time before I lose my nerve."

With a torch in one hand and his snare in the other, Luis led the way back into the caves. Within two minutes, he jerked to a halt. *"Allí! Un pequeno uno."*

"What?"

Without taking his eyes off the diamondback, Luis said, "There. A little one." Moving slowly, he lay his torch on the cave floor. Suddenly, the dark silence erupted with the sound that never failed to send shivers down Josh's spine—the chattering buzz of rattles.

"Easy, Luis," Leeboy whispered.

Luis deftly laid the loop of the rattler's head and whipped it tight. In the same motion, he lifted the snare and swung it slowly around. "The bag. Open wide."

Despite the chill of the cave, sweat rolled down Josh's face, stinging his eyes. "Just make sure you get it in the sack, boy," he muttered, holding the mouth of the bag as wide as he could.

With practiced skill, Luis lowered the diamondback tail first into the bag. He nodded. "Close bag," he said, releasing one of the deerskin strands and slipping the staff from the closed neck of the bag.

Josh quickly tied the bag tight. He grinned at Luis. "That worked fine, boy. Just fine."

Within an hour, they had filled the first bag with five snakes. "We'll leave this bag here. Pick it up on the way back. Now all we need are three more, one for each of the trails leading into their camp."

With a sardonic laugh, Leeboy said, "Now, I want to see how you plan on dangling them snakes."

Ignoring Leeboy's sarcasm, Josh looked at Luis. "Before you put the next snake in the bag, hold it up so I can tie a length of rawhide around its tail. The end of the rawhide will hang outside of the bag when we drop the snake in it." He grinned around at Leeboy. "Then all we'll have to do is pull one strand of rawhide at a time out of the bag and on the other end is our snake."

Leeboy lifted an eyebrow. "Sounds simple enough. That kinda worries me."

Josh ignored his red-headed friend. He motioned to Luis. "Let's go, Luis."

Five minutes later, Josh had the chance to put his theory to work. Luis held a five-foot rattler high above their heads. "Hold tight to that snake. And hold him

high." He grabbed the wiggling tail of the rattler, hesi-
tating momentarily when he felt the wiry muscles
beneath the cold, slick skin.

"Well?" Leeboy drawled. "You just going to hold
hands with it?"

Josh blinked once, then quickly slipped a loop over the
length of the rattles to the last button and tightened snugly. Stepping back, he opened the bag. "Put him in, boy."

With a broad smile that shone brightly in the torch-
light, Luis lowered the struggling snake, and Josh
quickly tied the bag tight, leaving five feet of rawhide
dangling from the throat of the bag. He gave Leeboy a
smug grin. "Like you said, partner. Simple."

Thirty minutes later, they were back in the first
chamber with two bags of rattlesnakes, both surpris-
ingly inactive. "Now," Josh said, studying the two
lumpy bags, "how do we haul them on the horses?"

"A travois," Leeboy said. "Rig up a travois. Simple."

"Why not?" Josh replied. "A simple answer from a
simple jasper. That'll work just fine."

Building a travois was an effortless process of tying
a few branches between the ends of two fifteen-foot
poles and joining the other ends with a three-foot strand
of rope, which was then strung over the horse's rump
and fastened to the saddle with the leather ties.

Snugging the two bags tightly to the platform of
branches, they headed upriver.

*   *   *

At noon, two miles downriver from the Union camp, Josh settled Luis and the diamondbacks in a small cave. "We'll be back before dark. We need to pull out as soon as the sun sets. We'll have to work fast. The moon will be rising early tonight."

Back outside, Leeboy and Josh led their ponies up a switchback trail to the caprock.

Staying well away from the rim of the caprock overlooking the corral, they gathered dried juniper and tumbleweeds, the latter tinder dry. Despite the fact the brittle tumbleweeds broke at the slightest touch, they managed to compress half-a-dozen or so in the middle of three bundles of dried juniper branches and tie them tightly.

Everywhere they looked on the caprock, they spotted dry tumbleweeds, so they gathered all within a hundred yards. They had a stack five feet high and twenty long.

"Don't knock anything over the edge and spook the horses," Josh cautioned Leeboy.

"I ain't the one with the big feet."

When they finished, Leeboy dropped to his hands and knees. "I want to see what the corral looks like so I'll know where to drop the fire."

Josh remained behind while Leeboy eased forward, fell to his belly, removed his hat, and peeked over the rim. He studied the corral, then hastily scooted back. "Easy," he said, climbing to his feet. "A straight drop."

"All right. Tonight after dark, move all this to the

rim. It'll burn fast, so when you hear the commotion, kick it down."

With the setting of the sun, the three, carrying their bags of snakes, left the cave and rode within a quarter-mile of the camp. They dismounted and tied their horses in a thick cluster of cottonwood. Josh looked at Leeboy. He stuck out his hand. "You be careful now, you hear? We'll meet right back here after the commotion."

Leeboy patted his pocket with his free hand. "You're the one who'd best take care. Me, I got my good luck charm."

The two friends held their hand clasp another few seconds, looking into each other's eyes. Finally Josh said, "Last one back here buys the first round of drinks."

"Be counting out your money then." Leeboy laughed softly and headed up the trail to the caprock.

Josh and Luis each carried a bag. When they spotted the campfire, they halted. "Wait here." He hefted his bag of five diamondbacks. "I want to put these fellers where I can get to them right fast. Then we'll rig up our other surprises."

Like the shadows themselves, Josh eased through the night until he reached the copse of cottonwoods where he would later meet Emmeline. He placed the bag at the base of a giant cottonwood and returned to Luis.

"Ready?" he whispered.

The young Mexican nodded. *"Si."*

"Let's go. And be careful."

Keeping their eyes on the camp, they crept up the first trail and strung a length of rawhide head high from one cottonwood to another on the opposite side of the trail. Josh picked up one of the rawhide cords dangling from the neck of the bag and slipped it over the taut rawhide spanning the trail. He tugged on the end, tightening the leather strand. "Lift the bag," he whispered, continuing to keep the leather tight. "Loosen the bag just a bit."

Moments later, a string of rattles popped out, and Josh quickly tied off his end of the leather to a low branch of a nearby juniper. "Don't move yet. Let me grab the other two rawhide strips. We don't want one of those fellers to pop out accidentally." He came around beside Luis and picked up the two loose strips of leather. "All right, pull the bag away."

And when Luis did as Josh instructed, the diamondback slipped out of the bag and swung back and forth in the air, twisting its wiry body in an effort to free itself.

"Yep," Josh muttered. "That'll work just fine. Now, let's take care of the other two trails."

Fifteen minutes later, they had completed their job and returned to the copse of cottonwoods where Josh had stashed the bag of rattlesnakes. "Stay here, and stay hidden," he cautioned Luis. "When I get back, we'll have to get out of here faster than a grasshopper out of a chicken yard. So, you be here, and you be ready."

Luis nodded, watching silently as Josh picked up the bag and disappeared into the night. He glanced at the campfire around which the soldiers squatted, drinking coffee and laughing. Emmeline Terry sat several feet from the fire, her eyes searching the shadows around the camp.

Josh crouched behind a boulder a few feet from where Zeke's men had rolled out their bedrolls. He untied the neck of the bag, then picked up a small stone and tossed it beyond the campfire.

The small rock struck with a sharp click, causing the men around the fire to look in that direction. Josh jumped to his feet, swung the bag around his head once, and heaved it at the fire. The bag hit directly in the middle of the flames, exploding coals in every direction.

"What the—" one of the men said, turning back to the fire, only to see five furious rattlesnakes pouring from the mouth of the bag.

Shrieks of terror, punctuated by gunfire, ripped the night apart. The Union cavalrymen broke in every direction. Josh darted for the cottonwoods, where he waited impatiently for Emmeline.

Moments later, she raced into the cluster of cottonwoods. Josh grabbed her hand. "This way, and don't slow down."

As soon as Leeboy heard the gunfire and shouting from below, he touched a match to the juniper bundles.

When the tumbleweeds inside the bundle caught, he kicked the fireballs over the rim. Hastily, he ignited the remaining tumbleweeds and sent them bouncing down the side of the caprock into the corral.

Then he spun on his heel and raced down the trail to the river.

The night was a cacophony of screams and gunshots, quickly joined by the squealing of frightened horses escaping the mass of fire falling down upon them.

Josh raced through the cottonwoods back to where they had picketed their ponies. Despite lungs burning from running, he grinned. Their plan had worked to perfection.

The camp was in an uproar. Without warning, terri-fied horses stampeded across the campfire and vanished into the darkness beyond.

Young Luther Webb screamed, "Snake, snake, snake!" and, panicking, burst out running down the trail, trying desperately to put as much distance as he could between himself and the snakes.

He never saw the diamondback hanging in the mid-dle of the trail, but he felt the burning pain in his neck.

Screaming, Private Serra scrambled up on a boulder while Sergeant Kincaid stood unmoving, coolly shoot-ing one twisting, writhing rattlesnake after another.

Corporal Crocker was luckier than young Webb for he spotted the diamondback hanging in the middle of the trail down which he was running. With a grim curse, he unloaded his Colt into the snake, the last shot blowing its head off.

Then he plopped down on a boulder and shook with fear.

Zeke Tanner cursed at the confusion. He still wasn't quite certain just what had happened or how it had happened, but there was no question in his mind who was behind it. And until he figured out a way to handle those two, his plan to steal the Confederate gold for himself was wrapped up tighter than bark on an oak tree.

Leeboy was waiting for them when they reached the horses. "Looks like you buy the drinks, partner."

Josh helped Emmeline up behind Leeboy and swung into his saddle. He had just pulled Luis up behind him when he heard Zeke's voice drifting down the river. "Josh! Leeboy! I know you're out there. Let's talk."

Both men remained silent.

Zeke continued. "We'll work out a deal. Remember the old times. Come on in. Let's talk it out."

Josh shook his head and reined his bay around. Leeboy followed. "The old times, he says," Leeboy sneered.

Chapter Fifteen

Zeke Tanner stared into the darkness, cursing. His only course of action now was to continue the pretense of heading for La Junta until he could find a way to shake Leeboy and Josh from his tail. He glanced around, spotting Private Jorge Serra still crouched on the boulder. "Serra! Round up our horses. Crocker! Where are you?"

A thin voice drifted up one of the trails. "Here I am, Lieutenant."

"Give Serra a hand with the horses."

"Someone done set up a trap for us on this trail, Lieutenant," Crocker called back. "They done hung a rattlesnake across the trail. Lucky I spotted it, or I'd be deader'n a beaver hat."

"Hold on, Serra!" Tanner barked. Frowning, he

131

shook his head, half in anger, half in admiration for his two old friends' methods. "Private Serra. You and Crocker check the other trails from the camp. Make sure they're safe."

In the meantime, Sergeant Kincaid rebuilt the fire, the leaping flames of which cast its light down the trails. Tanner remained at the edge of the firelight, peering into the darkness. Kincaid came up behind him. "Old friends, huh, Lieutenant?"

With a wry grunt, Tanner grimaced. "Used to be."

"What's this deal you told him you'd make?"

Looking around slowly, Tanner grinned coldly. He tilted the muzzle of his handgun. "This."

Kincaid chuckled. "My kind of deal."

At that moment, a gunshot rang out from down one trail. Serra called out, "Rattlesnake down here, Lieutenant. He's dead now."

"What about it, Crocker?" Tanner peered down the third trail.

"No snake, Lieutenant, but I found Luther. He's dead."

"Snakebite?"

"Can't tell. Too dark."

Quickly, Lieutenant Tanner picked up a torch and hurried down the trail. Young Luther Webb lay curled on his side, his hand clutching his neck. Tanner held the torch up, lighting the strand of rawhide stretched across the trail. Carefully, he searched the area, but there was no sign of the rattler.

He squatted and pulled Luther's hand from his throat. He grimaced at the two bloody holes in the young private's carotid artery, bringing death within seconds. "Grab his arms, Private. I'll grab his legs. We'll carry him back to camp and bury him before we pull out."

"Yes, sir."

As Lieutenant Tanner hefted young Luther Webb's legs, a strange sense of relief came over him. Now, he didn't have to wonder if he could have actually killed the young man. Josh Miles and Leeboy Strauss had done his job for him. Maybe he should thank them.

As Josh and Leeboy rode south, Luis spotted two horses watering at the river's edge. He tugged on Josh's shirt. "Look. Horses. We ride now."

Reining up, Josh motioned Leeboy to continue beyond the horses. "Think you can get them without spooking them, boy?"

Luis slid off the bay. *"Si."* He jabbed a finger into his chest. "I am good with horses like I am with *las serpientes.*"

The cavalry remounts looked up as Luis slowly approached, cooing unintelligible sounds. They stood motionless, ears forward, staring at him. Slowly, gently, he eased between them and gently grasped a tuft of hair beneath each animal's cheek.

Josh watched in amazement as the horses docilely permitted the young Mexican to lead them. Leeboy whistled softly, "You got some knack there, Luis."

Quickly slicing off two lengths of his lariat, Josh rigged halters. "Let's head across the river here and find a spot in the ridges to figure out our next step." He glanced at Emmeline. "Think you can ride some?"

She stared at him, anxiously wanting to ask the myriad questions tumbling about in her head, but she simply slid off Leeboy's horse and nodded. "Yes." She reached between her ankles and clutched the back hem of her dress. She pulled it up between her legs and tucked it into her waistband, effectively turning her billowing dress into a pair of trousers.

Leeboy arched an eyebrow at Josh as if to say, 'would you look at that?'

Thirty minutes later, they found a shallow arroyo protected by ridges on either side. They paused to rest, to refresh themselves before continuing in the dark.

While Luis kept lookout from the top of the ridge, Josh introduced the three of them to Emmeline Terry. He explained how they'd found her father and brother, buried them, and then continued the pursuit. "We got here as fast as we could. Are you all right? Did they hurt you?"

Starlight glittered on the tears rolling down her cheeks. She shook her head. "The lieutenant was very firm with the men. I think he would have killed one had they touched me."

Leeboy looked at Josh, and the two nodded at each other. "At least Zeke ain't turned mean toward women."

"Yep. At least."

A frown knit her brows. "You talk like you know him." Her tone was accusing.

With a frown sliding over his face, Leeboy nodded. "Once upon a time. He ain't the same man we knew."

Emmeline looked from Leeboy to Josh and back. Josh cleared his throat. "We grew up together. Lost touch around nine years back. Like Leeboy said, he isn't the same Zeke Tanner we knew."

Leeboy looked around. "So, now what? Take Miss Emmeline back?"

His voice filled with resignation, Josh replied, "Reckon so. That's about the only choice we got. Maybe we could find a spot to leave her and Luis."

Leeboy arched an eyebrow. "But what if something happens to you and me? They'll be—"

"Just a minute," Emmeline interrupted, her voice firm. Surprised, they looked at her as she continued, "What would you do if I wasn't here?"

Leeboy shrugged. "Why, that's easy. We'd stay closer to Zeke than two coats of paint."

She looked at Josh, and he nodded his agreement. "Then," she said, "let's do it." Before either could protest, she explained. "I'm not one of those little frail, puny town girls. I grew up on a ranch, worked cattle with my pa and brother, shot mountain lions, and during the winter, killed rabbits and deer for food. Those animals back there killed my brother and father. I want to make sure they get what they deserve."

Leeboy and Josh exchanged perplexed looks. Finally, Leeboy shrugged. "Why not?"

A broad grin played over Josh's face. "Why not?"

"What do we do now, follow Zeke?"

Josh peered into the darkness toward the camp. "I don't reckon he'll hang around over yonder much longer. He's got the gold. I got me a hunch we figured right the other day about where he's headed."

"Colorado?"

"Yep. La Junta."

A slow grin played over Leeboy's freckled face. "Then why don't we ride up ahead and plan a surprise for old Zeke and his blueboys when they show up?" He looked around at Emmeline. "You say you can shoot?"

Her jaw set, she said, "Better than my brother or pa."

"Good. But, I don't want you and the boy with us when the shooting starts." Emmeline parted her lips to protest, but Josh continued. "No argument. We'll find a cave in the caprock where you and Luis can take shelter. Take a rifle in case you need it." He looked at Leeboy.

The red-headed cowpoke nodded emphatically. "You bet. Lead plums could be humming around like bees."

"But, I can help," she argued.

"Me too," Luis protested.

"You can help us best by doing what we ask," Leeboy said. "If you two was with us, Miss Emmeline, you wouldn't want us to, but we'd have to pay attention to you instead of giving it all to those Union boys. If we had to skedaddle, you'd slow us down. I hope you understand what I mean."

She remained silent a few moments, then nodded. "All right. I'll do what you ask." She glanced at Luis crouched behind a juniper on the crest of the ridge. "We'll both do as you ask."

For a moment, Luis remained motionless. Finally, with disappointment etching a frown over his dark face, he nodded.

Leeboy pulled up beside her and dipped his head to her horse. "You want my saddle, Miss Emmeline? Bareback is kinda hard on the—" He hesitated, blushed. "I mean—"

She laughed softly. "I know what you mean. Thank you, but no. Most of my riding was bareback. I'm fine."

Josh grinned at Leeboy, glanced at Luis, then back to Emmeline Terry. If nothing else, he'd met a couple of mighty interesting folks on this trip.

Kincaid and Serra buried Luther Webb in a shallow grave while Crocker herded the horses back in the corral. "I could only find four of our mounts, Lieutenant," he said.

Sergeant Kincaid wiped the sweat from his forehead with the back of his hand. The firelight cast nebulous shadows over his face. "That means two of us got to carry another saddlebag of gold, Lieutenant."

Tanner, who had been gazing southward in the direction Josh and Leeboy had disappeared, looked around and grimaced, realizing an extra sixty or so pounds would wear a horse down right fast. "Looks like we'll have to take turns carrying the bags. Private Serra, you and Crocker throw an extra saddlebag on your remounts. After a couple of hours, the sergeant and I'll spell you."

Wordlessly the two men nodded.

"Now," Tanner continued, turning back to the south and staring into the night, "put on the coffee. Get some rest."

Kincaid cleared his throat. "We're not staying put are we, Lieutenant?"

Serra glanced up in surprise at Sergeant Kincaid's questioning of the lieutenant's decision.

Without turning to face the sergeant, he replied in a soft, thoughtful voice, "For the moment."

"What if those two friends of yours come back?" The sarcastic emphasis he placed on the word, friends, was not lost on Zeke Tanner.

"That, Sergeant, is my business," he answered sharply.

For several seconds, Kincaid glared at Tanner's back. With a snort of disgust, he said, "Yes, sir," and turned away.

Corporal Crocker arched an eyebrow at Kincaid as the sergeant approached the fire. "What are you looking at, Corporal?" Kincaid snapped.

Crocker dropped his eyes. "Nothing, Sergeant. Ain't looking at nothing."

"Good. Just keep looking at nothing, and you and me will get along just fine," he said, shaking out his blankets.

A faint smile twisted Tanner's lips as he heard the exchange between the two enlisted men, but quickly faded as his thoughts returned to Leeboy and Josh. Those two weren't quitters. As boys, none of the three had known the meaning of the word, quit. The gimpy old Cherokee had taught them the value, the beauty of perseverance and what the trait could accomplish.

With a terse nod of his head, he knew they would be back. So now the questions Zeke Tanner had to answer were should he wait for them or should he pull out?

Gazing north, he wondered about Gian-nah-tah and Black Fox. When would they return? Or would they? Behind him, he heard the soft mumbling of his remaining three men. He knew he could kill them now and then Gian-nah-tah and Black Fox when they returned. If they returned. But still, there was Josh and Leeboy.

For the next two hours, Josh led the small party to the northwest, figuring Zeke and his patrol would follow the river to the head of the Palo Duro. Josh pointed to the ghostly silhouette of the caprock rising from the darkness. "Best I can remember the lay of the country thereabouts, La Junta is about a week's ride due north."

"How many men does Zeke have?"

"I saw five."

"What about the Indians?"

He shook his head. "Never saw them."

Leeboy's forehead wrinkled in a frown. "That don't make sense. Where do you reckon they went?"

"Can't say. Scouting maybe. Maybe they did the job Zeke hired them for and left."

As they drew close to the river, Leeboy cleared his throat. "Them Injuns not accounted for raises the hackles on the back of my neck, partner. Only thing worse than facing an Injun is not being able to face one when you know he could be out there."

Back to the east, false dawn crept above the horizon. Josh surveyed the countryside. "We best find us a place to hunker down and wait. If Zeke pulls out, it'll be before the sun shows its face."

"That ain't a bad spot over there," Leeboy said. "Where the river runs between those two ridges. If we get behind the one north of the river, we'll have the caprock at our back."

Josh studied the terrain. The ridge was high enough so if Zeke and his patrol remained on the north side of the river, they would pass directly below the crest. There was no shelter for them for a hundred yards in any direction. "Looks good to me." He pointed to the ridge. "Let's find a cave for Miss Emmeline and Luis. Then we can dig us a little hole up there on top of the ridge we can hunker down in."

Luis spoke up. "I know of cave." He gestured to the caprock. When he saw the frown on Josh's face, he explained, "I come here with Comanche."

Chapter Sixteen

A half-mile to the south on the side of another ridge, two Indians sat motionless on their war ponies behind a copse of juniper, watching impassively as the four members of the small party rode to the base of the caprock, left the woman and boy in a cave, and returned to a high ridge overlooking the river. The two cowboys picketed their horses at the bottom of the ridge, then, rifles in hand, climbed to the top and plopped down on their bellies overlooking the river.

Black Fox looked up at the large Apache, his eyes asking the question. Gian-nah-tah grunted. "They wait."

"Soldiers?" Black Fox looked back around, his keen eyes pinpointing the two positions on the ridge.

Gian-nah-tah backed his pony down the ridge. "Come. We go to soldiers."

The Comanche warrior jabbed his heels into his pony's flanks. Within seconds, both horses were in a full gallop. Gian-nah-tah made a wide circle, staying out of both sight and hearing of the men dug in on the crest of the ridge.

He wasn't sure what was taking place, but whatever it was, it would not stop him from taking his share of the gold. From the corner of his eye, he saw Black Fox urging his pony faster. An evil leer twisted his scarred face. Maybe he'd even take the Comanche's share as well.

"I'm getting sore laying in one spot so long," Leeboy growled. "What do you figure Zeke's doing?"

"We have only been here an hour or so," Josh replied, glancing at the sun about two hands' width above the horizon. "Even if he pushed out before sunrise, it'll be around mid-morning." He rolled over and sat up. "Hand me the canteen."

Mid-morning, Zeke Tanner jerked around at Private Serra's shout. "The Injuns, Lieutenant! They're coming in."

Wearing a sullen expression, Gian-nah-tah reined up and stared down at Tanner.

"Well, see any Comanche or Kiowa?"

With an almost imperceptible nod, Gian-nah-tah said, "Many. Like the stars. The young ones, their blood is hot. The old ones find it difficult to keep them from war."

"How far?"

"One time the sun comes and returns."

Kincaid had come to stand behind Tanner. "One day. Too close for me."

Keeping his eyes on the two Indians, Lieutenant Tanner pondered the information. "You're right, Sergeant. They're not far, but far enough so we can slip past them."

"How do you plan on that, Lieutenant? If I might ask," he added quickly, remembering the scathing rebuke from the previous night.

Tanner turned to Kincaid. A slight smile curled one side of his lips. "Half a day northeast of here, Sergeant, a branch canyon runs about forty miles northward. That's forty miles less of flat, treeless caprock we'll have to cross. From there, La Junta is four days." What he didn't say was the branch canyon was initially where he planned on carrying out the last step of his plan, the plan Josh and Leeboy had thrown into disarray. He looked past the sergeant at his men. "Saddle up, boys. We're moving out."

"Ambush up river," the scar-faced Apache muttered flatly as if he was announcing he was going to take a nap.

The three words stopped Tanner in his tracks. He jerked around. "Ambush?"

Black Fox spoke. "Two men. One woman. Small Indian boy."

A woman! Instantly, Zeke Tanner knew Black Fox was speaking of Josh and Leeboy. He grimaced, and then a slow grin erased the scowl. He figured those two would try something, but an ambush, especially with the woman, was the last thing he would have guessed. He studied the Comanche. "You sure they had a woman?"

"Me see. They hide her and boy in cave, then climb up on ridge."

He glanced at Gian-nah-tah who nodded his agreement. "How far?"

The massive Apache looked into the sky and pointed straight up.

"About two hours," Tanner told his men, translating the Apache's reply. He knelt and in the sand, drew a line indicating the river. He pointed to it. "*Dónde? Where?*"

Gian-nah-tah squatted and extended the line in the sand on an angle to the left, then back right to run between the two ridges, which he represented with two more lines in the sand, one on either side of the river. He pointed to the line on the north side. "They hide there."

Tanner's eyes glittered. His old boyhood chums had made a mistake. With luck, it was the mistake that would put Tanner's plans back on track. Looking up, he indicated the rim of the caprock above, then pointed to the line representing the ridge on which they hid.

Gian-nah-tah frowned, but Black Fox understood immediately. Kneeling, he drew a line behind the ridge to indicate the proximity of the caprock.

Nodding slowly, Tanner quickly formulated a plan. "Here's what we'll do. Gian-nah-tah and Black Fox will travel on the caprock. The rest of us will stay on the north shore of the river." He turned to the two Indians. "Is there a trail coming down from the caprock?"

Gain-nah-tah gave a single nod. "Many."

Tanner's lips twisted into a thin, cruel grin. "When the shooting starts, you get the woman and boy. That'll throw cold water on those two jasper's hot blood."

"We kill woman and boy?" Black Fox's eyes glittered with expectation.

"No." Tanner laid his hand on the butt of his revolver. "I'll kill anyone who hurts her or the boy." He paused. "Any questions?" He looked each man in the eyes. There were none. "All right then. Mount up."

While Lieutenant Tanner cinched down his saddle, Gian-nah-tah rode up beside him. Speaking under his breath, he said, "When is my share of gold?"

For a fleeting moment, Tanner hesitated, and then, his tone brusque, replied, "Two days. That is when we will reach the gold. Then you will have your share."

The Apache grunted, and falling in behind Black Fox, headed up to the caprock.

The August sun baked the canyon. In the distance, waves of rising heat distorted the terrain, giving the illusion the countryside was rolling like waves in the sea.

On the ridge, Leeboy, his hat pulled over his eyes, napped. Josh watched downriver, his vigilance dulled by the debilitating heat and hours of seeing nothing.

Suddenly, he jerked alert and squinted into the early

afternoon haze. Sure enough, riders were coming. Zeke! He shook Leeboy awake. "Wake up, son. Here they come."

Leeboy didn't move.

Josh looked around at him. "Did you hear me?"

A muffled drawl replied, "I heard you, but I hated to leave that darling little girl."

Turning his attention back to the approaching riders, Josh said, "What little girl?"

"Why, that little girl I had my arm around in my dream."

Josh snorted.

Leeboy continued, still motionless. "Yep. A cold beer in one hand and a darling little girl in the other. And then you come along and jerk me away from her." He slid his hat back from his eyes and grinned up at Josh. "Some friend you claim to be."

Flexing his fingers about his Henry, Josh said, "You help me take of business here, and I'll buy you that beer."

"I'll hold you to that." He rolled over and peered over the crest of the ridge. "About ten minutes," he muttered.

The next few minutes dragged. Josh forced himself to breathe slowly. "Get ready." He snuggled the butt of his Henry into his shoulder and touched his finger to the trigger.

Leeboy glanced toward the cave where they left Emmeline and Luis. "Josh! Look yonder." He pointed to a trail descending the caprock. "Indians."

For a moment Josh studied the Indians. From their dress, he saw one was Comanche and the larger one was Apache. His brain raced. What were they up to? He glanced back at the patrol. "You think maybe they're just riding by?"

Leeboy licked his lips. His gaze shifted from the two Indians to the approaching patrol. "I don't think so," he replied, his voice grim, and his gaze shifting back to the two warriors. "I'll bet you that beer them are the two Indians scouting for Zeke."

"That's one bet I won't take."

"What do we do?"

The patrol was still beyond range of their Henry rifles. Josh tore his eyes away from the approaching riders and focused on the two Indians. "We'll find out what they got in mind when they reach the bottom of the cliff. You watch them. I'll keep my eyes on Zeke."

Muttering a soft curse, Josh laid his cheek on the stock and lined the sight on Zeke. He thought he had out-slicked his old friend, but it turned out to be the other way around. How in the Sam Hill had Zeke learned about their trap?

When the two Indians reached the base of the caprock, instead of heading directly for the ridge, they turned left with the Apache in the lead. Leeboy's voice was taut with alarm. "Blast it, Josh. They're heading for the cave! We've got to get over there!"

Josh's finger tightened on the trigger, but the distance

was still too great, and with every second, the Indians were drawing closer to the cave.

With a blasphemous oath, Josh jumped to his feet and raced down the ridge to his bay, his head filled with frustrated anger at how their plans had fallen apart, and a gripping fear for the safety of Emmeline Terry and Luis Alvarado Elizio Guadalupe Martinez.

He swung into the saddle and dug his spurs into the bay. The juniper and mesquite blurred as he, with Leeboy's horse matching his bay stride for stride, raced toward the cave in a desperate effort to cut off the two Indians. Leaning low over the neck of his pony, Leeboy shouted, "Zeke'll spot us when we get out from behind the ridge."

Josh clenched his teeth and set his jaw, keeping his eyes on the Indians, who had now kicked their horses into a gallop in an attempt to intercept them.

As he shot from behind the ridge, Josh threw a hasty glance over his shoulder at the patrol, which, as soon as it spotted Josh and Leeboy, dug it spurs in, sending the horses racing after the two fleeing cowpokes.

Patting his bay's neck; Josh tightened his legs about his pony's chest and whispered, "Faster, boy, faster." The wind whipped his face as the bay surged forward, lengthening his strides, eating up the ground.

The dark mouth of the cave beckoned.

Leeboy shouted, "It's going to be close, Josh!"

Off to their left came the report of gunshots. In front of Josh, a chunk of rock exploded. He leaned lower over his pony's neck, not as worried about the accuracy of the Indians' shots as much as a random slug finding its mark. Indian rifles were notorious for inaccuracy.

But, to stack the cards in his favor, he shucked his sixgun and threw a wild shot in the direction of the Indians. He knew he could not hope to hit them at this distance. He'd be lucky to hit the side of the caprock, but a shot might make them a little more cautious.

He glanced to his right. He and Leeboy had about a hundred-yard lead on Zeke and his men who, to Josh's surprise, had not fired a shot. The Apache was another matter. Sitting erect in his grass saddle, he was firing as fast as he could lever cartridges into the chamber.

"We're not going to make it!" shouted Leeboy, slipping his Colt from the holster and pointing the muzzle toward the two red savages who were about the same distance from the mouth of the cave as Josh and Leeboy.

By now, they had closed the distance to the galloping Indians so now Josh could hear the war cries above the roar of gunfire. "Let's surprise them!" he yelled, waving the muzzle on his .44 Army Colt toward the oncoming Indians.

Leeboy frowned, then grinned when he realized Josh's intentions. With a wild shout of his own, he jerked his horse straight for the two Indians. Josh was at his side, and the two started emptying their Colts at the startled Indians, who, thrown off balance by the unexpected charge, reined up and tried to return fire.

The murderous hail of lead knocked Black Fox from his saddle and forced Gain-nah-tah to turn and run.

Holstering their Colts, Leeboy and Josh swerved for the cave, twenty-five yards distant. By now, Zeke was less than fifty yards behind.

Chapter Seventeen

"**J**osh! Leeboy! Might as well come out. You're not going anywhere." Zeke pressed his back to the red claystone rock next to the mouth of the cave. Kincaid was at his side. Crocker and Serra stood on the other side of the cave opening. He knew this cave well from the year he had spent living in Palo Duro Canyon. It twisted and curled under the caprock, coming out half a mile upriver. "We can wait longer than you."

From the darkness in the cave, Josh shouted back, "Then wait! The longer you stay here, the longer you blueboys can't use the gold."

Tanner looked at Crocker and Serra. "You men gather dry wood. We'll smoke them out."

Kincaid grinned.

Inside, Josh peered around the corner of a bend and

watched the stack of dried wood grow larger and larger in the mouth of the cave.

"What are they doing?" Leeboy whispered.

His tone grim, Josh replied, "He plans to smoke us out."

Emmeline caught her breath.

Luis tugged on Josh's sleeve. "There is a way out."

"What?" Leeboy exclaimed.

The peripheral light from the cave's mouth offered miniscule illumination. Luis nodded. "When I come here with Comanche last winter, we stay in caves. Stay warm."

"And you've been in this one?" Josh asked in stunned disbelief at their sudden stroke of fortune.

"*Si.* Many times." He pointed into the darkness. "There are many openings."

"What about our horses? We're up against it out here without our horses," Leeboy said.

"*Si.* Much room for horses."

By now, half of the cave's mouth was filled with dry wood.

Tanner's voice echoed down the shadowy tunnel. "Leeboy, Josh. Last chance. Come on out or we'll smoke you out."

Leeboy winked at Josh. "Smoke away, Copperhead." He looked down at Luis. "We need torches."

"I can help," Emmeline said. "You can use my petticoat."

Josh pulled out his knife. "Thanks, but no need. We'll cut up a blanket."

At that moment, a flaming torch arched through the air into the middle of the stack of dried wood. Quickly, the flames began eating into the tinder-dry branches. The first tendrils of smoke curled back into the cave.

Having no branches to wrap the strips of blanket around, Josh draped a strip over the barrel of each of their rifles. "When it burns, just slap another one over the barrel, but first, empty the magazine and chamber of your Henry. Don't want the heat from the torch to set off the cartridges."

Quickly, both cowpokes emptied their rifles of cartridges. Josh looked around. "Ready?"

"I am," said Emmeline.

Josh touched a match to each end of the strip draped over the barrel. "Luis and I'll go first. Miss Emmeline, you come behind, and Leeboy'll bring up the rear."

"Wait a minute," Leeboy said.

The others looked at him. "What?"

He fixed his eyes on Luis. "Snakes. Are there snakes in here?"

With the casual nonchalance of familiarity, Luis replied, "Oh, *si, si, las serpientes* here."

Leeboy gulped. "That ain't what I wanted to hear," he muttered, laying his hand on the lucky gold eagle in his pocket.

The smoke grew thicker. Emmeline coughed. Josh looked down at the Mexican. "Show us the way, boy."

Outside, the fire raged. Smoke filled the mouth of the cave and curled up the side of the caprock. Lieutenant Tanner decided to take no chances. He sent Sergeant Kincaid and Private Serra to watch the second entrance upriver on the outside chance Josh might try to take them deeper into the labyrinths of the cave and somehow stumble across the exit.

Staring at the leaping flames, Corporal Crocker wiped the sweat from his forehead. "What do you think, Lieutenant?"

Tanner shrugged. "Those two jaspers, Corporal, are very resourceful." He gave Crocker a warning look. "Don't be surprised by anything. And stay away from the mouth of the cave. You're too good a target like that."

Crocker's forehead wrinkled in a frown. "Yes, sir, but how can they surprise us now? They're in the cave, and we got us a fire in the mouth. Looks to me we got 'em where we want 'em."

A wry grin played over Tanner's thin face. "That's the time to worry, Corporal. When you think you have someone where you want them."

The corporal arched a skeptical eyebrow. He said nothing, but from where he stood, there was nothing at all to worry about.

Tanner looked around as Gian-nah-tah swung into

his saddle. The heavily muscled Apache read the question in Tanner's eye. He pointed the muzzle of his rifle upriver. "I watch. Take no chances." He held out his right arm, extended his first two fingers and made a wavy, sinuous motion with his wrist. He nodded to the cave. "Those two white-eyes are like the snake. Not trust."

Nudging his warhorse with his heels, Gian-nah-tah put the pinto into a gentle lope along the river's edge. From time to time when he spotted a cave, he stepped inside and sniffed. He had been in the Canyon of Hardwood many times, and he knew the caves here were like the spider web.

Within minutes of heading farther into the damp cave, the darkness and the twists in the tunnel caused Josh to lose all sense of direction. As they progressed ever deeper, they passed tunnels branching off from the one they were in.

Once, Luis paused at a fork. He tilted Josh's torch to illuminate the red and yellow wall, on which two circles had been carved. He studied the markings, then set off to the left. Half a dozen steps down the left fork, the Mexican youth paused and indicated for Josh to hold his torch to the backside of an upthrust of red claystone.

The young Mexican peered at the wall, then grinned. "We go here," he said, entering a crevice behind the upthrust and stepping into a tunnel that led back in the direction from which they had come.

Concerned, Josh asked, "Are you certain we're heading in the right direction? Seems like we're doubling back on ourselves."

Without hesitation, Luis replied, "This one is best. The other, it goes back to river. This one leads to top."

"How long?" Leeboy's voice echoed off the rock walls.

"Not long."

The smoke followed them, sucked through the tunnels by the wind. From time to time, the astringent odor burned Josh's nostrils. Time passed slowly.

Gian-nah-tah smiled to himself as he stared at the cave opening two hundred feet up the side of the box canyon. A narrow trail led from the mouth of the cave to the canyon floor. He smelled wood smoke. He looked around. Thick with juniper and hackberry, the box canyon was a good place to hide. An inexplicable sense deep in his head told him this opening was the one from which those whom the lieutenant sought would emerge.

He reined about and headed back to the first cave.

Tanner eyed the Apache skeptically. He himself had explored this cave, and there were only two entrances. He would have bet the elephant on it. Still, over an hour had passed since he lit the fire. There was no sign of them here or at the second opening. Either they were lying dead inside, which he doubted, or they had discovered another branch of the cave. He decided to see for himself.

"I'll be back shortly, Crocker. Keep your eyes open," he said as he swung into the saddle.

Ten minutes later, he was studying the opening Giannah-tah had pointed out. He sniffed. The Apache was right. Wood smoke. He shook his head. A grudging smile played over his thin face. He knew if there were a way out of the trap, Josh and Leeboy would find it. It was a blasted shame the three of them weren't on the same side. His thoughts wandered momentarily, and then he came up with a daring idea. Maybe there was still time. A hundred thousand split three ways was still a heap of money.

Without warning, a muffled voice drifted down from above.

"Over there," Tanner whispered, quickly guiding his horse to a thick stand of juniper at the base of the caprock. The ledge above would shield them from view. He pulled his sidearm and cocked it.

After what seemed like hours to Josh, a light appeared ahead. "There," the young Mexican said.

"Sure looks good to me," yelped Leeboy. "Mighty good."

"*Cuidadoso*. Careful. The ledge in front of cave is—ah—*pequeno*. Small." He pointed downward. "Narrow trail go to ground. Comanche lead horse. Many have fallen."

Josh nodded. The Comanche were probably the greatest horsemen in all of the Indian tribes, and if they led their ponies down the trail, that's exactly what Josh and the others would do.

Pausing at the mouth of the cave to study the terrain surrounding them, Josh saw they were halfway up the side of the caprock in a box canyon that opened onto the main trunk of Palo Duro.

"Looks like we're out of sight back here," Leeboy noted. "At least we got room to fight Zeke." He looked around at their small group. "He's got three soldiers and the Apache. We can meet his firepower."

"Reload your Henry, and then let's get down there," said Josh, filling the magazine and levering a cartridge into the chamber.

When they reached the bottom of the trail, Josh swung into his saddle. After the others mounted, he said, "Miss Emmeline, you and Luis wait here while Leeboy and me scout the canyon. Let's see if we can find out what Zeke and his bluecoats are up to."

From where Zeke and Gian-nah-tah were hidden, they could plainly see the four riders. Gian-nah-tah eased his rifle to his shoulder, but Tanner stopped him. "Wait."

They watched as Josh and Leeboy rode from the box canyon. When they disappeared into the main canyon,

Tanner grinned at Gian-nah-tah. "Now we take the woman back."

Emmeline watched anxiously as Josh and Leeboy disappeared into the juniper and hackberry. The box canyon acted like an oven, catching and holding the sweltering heat of the blazing sun. She glanced at Luis, who looked up at her and grinned. "Do not worry. I am here."

The smile on her lips froze when she heard a rustling behind her. She jerked around just as Lieutenant Zeke Tanner emerged from the juniper. She turned to run, but stared into the leering smirk on the scarred face of Gian-nah-tah, who had seized her horse's halter. She screamed and looked for Luis, but all she saw was his horse. The boy had vanished.

Her terrified shriek cut through the still air lying over the riverbed. Josh and Leeboy jerked around, staring at each other in surprise—surprise that instantly turned to alarm. They yanked their ponies around and, digging spurs into their horses' flanks, raced back to the box canyon.

They slid to a halt when they burst through the juniper and spotted the grinning face of Zeke Tanner. In one hand, he held the reins of Emmeline's horse, and in the other, his Army Colt, the muzzle at her temple.

Chapter Eighteen

"Hello, boys," Zeke drawled, a thin sneer on his lips. "It's been an interesting chase."

Josh's blood ran cold. To his left, Gian-nah-tah, a cruel smile twisting his lips, slouched on his pinto. He held the muzzle of his Henry on them.

Muttering a soft curse, Leeboy placed both hands on his saddle horn and leaned forward. "You was always the daring one, Zeke, but you've gone too far this time." He nodded to Emmeline.

Deliberately, Tanner swung the muzzle of his Colt on Leeboy's chest. "You mean her?"

"Who else?"

Zeke feigned hurt feelings. "Now, Leeboy. I don't want you to think bad of your old friend. Why, I'm just doing my patriotic duty as I see it."

"Using a woman," Josh said scornfully. "I never figured you for that, Zeke."

Tanner's eyes narrowed. The sneer tightened on his lips. "Just doing whatever it takes for the cause."

Josh's brain raced. He couldn't afford to make a move now, not with a Henry on one side and Zeke Tanner holding a Colt on the other. "You got the drop now, Zeke. What's your play?"

Gesturing to their sidearms and rifles with the muzzle of his Colt, he replied good-naturedly, "First, old friends, drop your hardware. Then you're going to climb down and let my partner, Gian-nah-tah, tie your hands."

Leeboy bristled. "Ain't no man alive is going to wrap me up like spooked steer." He glared at Tanner defiantly. "You might have sunk low, Zeke Tanner, but not low enough to shoot me."

Tanner's sneer grew broader. "Oh, I won't kill you, Leeboy. For old time's sake, I won't kill you." His eyes grew cold and his voice brittle. "But I will bust your kneecaps so that you'll be on crutches the rest of your life." He jerked the Colt muzzle sharply toward the ground. "Now, climb down off that horse and squat. Both of you."

Josh growled between clenched teeth. "Do what the man says, Leeboy."

"You too, Miss Terry," Zeke said politely. He glanced at Luis' horse. "And call the boy in."

Emmeline glanced at Josh who nodded for her to do

as Tanner had ordered. She slid off her horse, and in a half-hearted effort, called Luis.

"Louder!" Zeke barked.

This time she cupped her hands to her lips and cried out at the top of her lungs. The echo of her voice bounced off the three canyon walls around them, but all they heard was the chirping of crickets in the hot silence.

Tanner studied the surrounding juniper. He dismissed the boy. "We'll get him later."

The heavily muscled Apache quickly bound Leeboy's and Josh's hands behind their backs where they had squatted. Zeke looked up at the scorching sun. He pointed to the shade at the base of the canyon wall. "Over there, boys, in the shade," drawled Zeke. "I don't want you to think I've no compassion." He nodded to Emmeline. "You too, Miss Terry. I'm not going to tie those pretty wrists of yours, but you sit yourself right down beside these two old boyhood chums of mine, and don't do a thing to make me regret not tying you up."

Tanner looked on warily as the three sat, Josh and Leeboy awkwardly with their hands behind their backs. Stepping back, he nodded to Gain-nah-tah. "Bring the others."

After the Apache disappeared into juniper, Zeke squatted and grinned at his old friends. "Sure wish this was under different set of circumstances, boys. I truly do. You have no idea how it pains me to see you all trussed up like this."

Leeboy sneered. "Yep, I can see you're crying mighty hard over it. You don't have the guts to take me on without a gun in your hand. You couldn't take care of me like you did JS."

"JS?" Tanner frowned. "Who are you talking about? I don't know any JS."

"JS Tipton," Josh snarled. "Our boss. The old man you hit in the barn."

Giving a brief shake of his head, Tanner said, "I didn't want to hit the old man, but I had no choice. He all right?"

"No, he ain't all right, Zeke!" Leeboy yelled. "You killed him."

For several moments, Tanner stared at Leeboy, then slowly shook his head. "Sorry, but he was in the way. I had no choice."

"Like you had no choice when you killed Miss Emmeline's brother and pa?"

Tanner glanced at Emmeline. "Exactly."

"But why? They weren't Army. It don't make sense," Leeboy added.

Josh spoke up. "Why'd you do it, Zeke? Why'd you turn Copperhead?"

Zeke Tanner stroked his chin, for a moment his eyes gazing through Josh. "Hard to say, Josh. I had no slaves. I couldn't see no sense fighting for them."

"Shoot, neither me or Leeboy got slaves, but you don't see us out fighting on one side or another, especially against our own."

"This whole war is about brothers and fathers fighting each other. At first, it made some sense."

"What do you mean, at first?"

Growing reflective, Zeke pushed to his feet and stared at the rim of the canyon high above. "I reckoned those who fought for the Confederacy wanted to keep the Negroes under their thumbs, like folks tried to do with me when I was a younker."

Josh and Leeboy looked at each other as Zeke continued. "After a spell of killing and more killing, I realized a war like this could go on forever. It'll go on until all of us are dead and only the rich and the politicians remain. So, I decided to do something about it."

"You talking about the Confederate gold for the invasion of Galveston?"

Zeke didn't answer immediately. He studied them with a gleam of amused cunning in his eyes.

Lifting an eyebrow, Zeke replied, "You're right when you talk about the gold, but, maybe you aren't right when you talk about the invasion of Galveston."

A frown knit Josh's eyebrows. "You lost me on that turn of the wheel, Zeke. You better spin it again."

He glanced sidelong at Emmeline, then took a step closer to Josh and Leeboy. He squatted so he was at eye level with them. He lowered his voice in a conspiratorial tone. "What if I told you the gold would never reach Union hands?"

Josh's frown deepened. He glanced at Leeboy who was equally puzzled. "What do you mean?"

Zeke shot a hasty look in the direction in which Gian-nah-tah had disappeared. He studied his two old friends, trying to decide if he should voice the daring idea that had flashed through his head only minutes earlier. *Why not*, he said to himself.

Fixing his eyes on them, he spoke slowly, deliberately. "I mean, the gold will never reach Union hands. I'm claiming it, and I'm willing to share it with you two."

His declaration shocked Leeboy and Josh speechless. Finally, Josh found his voice. "That's why you killed the old man and his son? Not for the Army, but for the gold?"

"I planned this for a long time. Shipments of gold are regularly made from Arizona Territory to Texas and beyond. This particular shipment of gold just happened to be the one that fit into my plan."

Josh's eyes narrowed. He cut his eyes in the direction Gian-nah-tah had disappeared. "All of you planned this?"

With a scornful sneer, Zeke snorted. "The others? They think the gold is going to La Junta, Colorado. The place is full of Union sympathizers."

Emmeline stared at Zeke in stunned disbelief as Leeboy inquired, "So what do you reckon your men are going to say when they learn the truth?"

His voice filled with disdain, Zeke said, "The men? I'll take care of them." He grinned. "You don't know it, but you've been a big help to me already, thanks to your little trick with the rattlesnakes. One of my men died." He paused, a strange glitter in his eyes as he continued in a flat, unemotional tone. "I shot one when the Kiowa attacked us, and I don't plan for any of the others to leave Palo Duro Canyon, not even the Apache."

Josh could only stare at Zeke, staggered by the cold-blooded audacity of his boyhood chum's plan.

Zeke continued, fervor in his voice. "There's a hundred thousand in gold. We'll split it three ways, over thirty thousand each. Enough for a nice ranch and a herd of prime beef with plenty left over."

Leeboy shook his head. "You're crazy, Zeke. You can't get away with this. The Army'll come after you."

Dark anger twisted Zeke's face for a fleeting second before relaxing into an amiable grin. "No, they won't." He glanced around the canyon. With a sly look, he said, "I planned this all very carefully. I spent a year living in Palo Duro. I know of caves that run for miles, that have underground springs. A man could live a lifetime here and never be seen."

Josh studied his old friend as he continued to elaborate on his plan. He realized Zeke had not changed as much as he had evolved from a mistrustful youth absorbed with the idea the world was against him to a man obsessed with taking from the world that which he believed belonged to him. No, Zeke hadn't changed. His youthful fears had simply intensified into twisted hatred.

Emmeline's eyes blazed. "You—you animal." Her words slashed at him.

A sneer twisted his lips. "Correction, Miss Terry. A rich animal."

From where she was sitting, Emmeline lunged at him, arms extended, her fingers like claws. Zeke simply jumped to his feet and let her sprawl face down on the hot claystone. "Try that again, and I'll hogtie you. Now get back over there and sit. And don't move a one of those pretty muscles."

Josh spoke up. "You didn't answer my question, Zeke."

"Oh?" He lifted an eyebrow. "And what question was that?"

"What are your men going to say when we tell them what you're really planning?"

He laughed. His tone filled with confidence, he replied, "They won't believe you. I'll tell them you're trying to create a conflict between us so you can take advantage of it. Who do you think they'll believe?"

Josh grimaced.

Leeboy struggled against the ropes binding his wrists and growled. "If I could get my hands on you just one more time, Zeke Tanner, I'd—"

Zeke interrupted, feigning a frown. "I take it then, you old boys don't plan on taking me up on my generous offer of going into partnership together." He shrugged indifferently. "Too bad. More for me, but unfortunately, I suppose that pretty well seals your fate." He grimaced and shook his head. "I don't much cotton to the idea, but I know you two well enough to realize you'll stay after me. I can't have that. So—"

The clatter of hooves on the hard claystone interrupted Zeke. He looked around as Gian-nah-tah emerged from the thick green juniper followed by Kincaid, Serra, and Crocker. Zeke looked at Josh, a taunting grin on his lips. "Go ahead, tell them. See what they say."

Kincaid frowned at the Lieutenant's remarks.

Josh remained silent, glaring at Zeke.

"Well, Josh. Go ahead. Here's your chance."

"I'll tell them," Leeboy blurted out. He looked up at the riders. "Zeke here plans on killing every last one of you fellers and taking the gold for himself. He's the one who killed your friend back when the Kiowas attacked." When he finished, he looked up at Zeke Tanner with smug satisfaction.

For several seconds, no one spoke. Sergeant Kincaid broke the silence. "What's the reb trying to do, Lieutenant?"

"Cause trouble. While you men were gone, these two Confederate sympathizers said they were going to make you think I wanted the gold for myself." As he spoke, he slowly turned to face his men, his revolver in hand, muzzle down. "They were hoping to create dissension among us. Split the force and conquer."

Josh saw the muzzle of Zeke's Colt slowly rising,

rising to center on Sergeant Frank Kincaid's chest. He parted his lips to shout a warning, but before he could utter a word, Private Jorge Serra shrieked in agony and toppled from his saddle, an arrow in his heart.

Chapter Nineteen

"What the—" Zeke spun and snapped off a shot toward the rim of the canyon. The dark silhouette of an Indian tumbled through the air, his dying scream ending abruptly when he slammed into the hard claystone floor of the canyon.

The sudden attack galvanized the men into action. Gian-nah-tah vanished into the juniper and hackberry only to return moments later. He pointed in the direction of the riverbed. "Comanche. War party. Many."

Zeke cursed and looked around, assessing his position, taking in the three canyon walls around him. "Could be worse," he muttered. "All right, men. Dismount. Picket your horses. Break out your rifles and take positions just inside the juniper trees. You can see them, but they can't see you." He glanced at the canyon rim above, but there were no Comanches in sight. Maybe the one was only a scout.

He hurried to the perimeter of the juniper and quickly counted twenty mounted Comanches. They were out of range, but they were riding hard, and they were riding straight for the box canyon.

Luck smiled on Zeke Tanner, for just as he turned, a rifle boomed and a lead slug slammed into one of the twisted juniper limbs at his side, ripping the limb apart with a sharp crack. He looked up as the Comanche hastily clacked another cartridge into the chamber. Before the Indian could manage to get off a second shot, Zeke heard the familiar boom of a Sharps and spotted a plume of smoke off to his right.

The impact of the slug knocked the Comanche backward off his feet.

The yelping howls of the charging Comanche echoed off the canyon walls as Zeke raced through the junipers and slid to a halt in front of Josh and Leeboy. He fished a knife from his pocket and slashed at their bonds. "I got no choice, boys. Either I turn you loose or the Comanches'll have all our scalps."

Josh scrambled to his feet and grabbed his Henry and Colt. "We got something to settle when this is over, Zeke. You know that, don't you?"

Zeke gave him a crooked grin. "Let's wait until it's over." He pointed the muzzle of his Colt at the rim. "Leeboy, you keep an eye peeled up there. Josh, you come with me."

"Wait!" Emmeline interrupted. They looked around at her. "Leeboy, you go with them." She glared defiantly at Zeke. "Give me a rifle. I'll watch the rim."

For a moment, Zeke hesitated, undecided.

Josh prodded him. "Well, give her one. I got a feeling not a single Comanche that sticks his scalp lock over the edge of the rim will have a chance to do it a second time."

Zeke unbooted the Henry he carried and tossed it to her. He turned to fish a box of cartridges from his saddlebags. "Here," he said, turning back to face Emmeline. He froze. She held the Henry waist high, one hand on the forearm, the other at the trigger. The dark hole in the end of the muzzle was centered on Zeke's chest.

The startled look on his face melted into a smirk. "You want to pull the trigger, Miss Terry, but you're too smart to do it now. Like it or not, we need each other. Here! Now get busy." He tossed her the box of cartridges, which she deftly caught.

By the time the three boyhood friends reached the perimeter of the juniper, the war party was splashing across the shallow river less than fifty yards distant. Dropping to one knee behind a thick juniper, Josh looked around to see Leeboy grinning at him. He nodded to the charging Comanches. "I figure we got to get four each."

Still grinning, Leeboy replied, "Blazes, Josh. Four to one? Why I reckon we got them outnumbered."

Josh set his jaw. From the corner of his eye, he saw Zeke. Regrets washed over him, but he pushed them aside.

"Steady, men!" Zeke called out. "Steady."

The Comanches stormed from the water. Josh could see them clearly now, leaning low over their war ponies, their long black hair streaming behind, a savage snarl on their painted faces.

"Now!"

As one, one Colt and five rifles boomed. Two Comanche tumbled over the croup of their ponies while three warhorses slid to the ground on their noses, spilling their riders.

The rifles boomed again.

By now, the Comanche were returning fire, aiming at the balloons of smoke from the muzzles of the Spencers and Henrys.

"Keep giving it to them, men! We've got to turn them!" Zeke shouted, standing upright in full view of the charging war party, firing his Colt slowly and deliberately.

Josh heard firing in the juniper beyond Zeke. The Apache, he guessed. He shouted above the clamor of the battle. "Blast it, Zeke! Get down!" A slug ricocheted off the claystone inches from Josh's foot. He muttered a curse and set the sights of his Henry on a leering Comanche who was sitting upright in the saddle and appeared to be aiming at Zeke. Josh didn't hesitate. He touched off the shot. The impact knocked the Comanche from his saddle. He bounced and rolled over when he hit the ground, then lay still.

A cry of pain came from the junipers to Josh's left. A voice called out over the din of the battle. "They got Crocker, Lieutenant."

Zeke muttered a curse and with his last shot, knocked a Comanche from the back of his pony. He jammed the big Colt under his belt and pulled out a second one.

By now, the lead warrior was less than twenty yards from the perimeter of the juniper, close enough that Josh could see the scowl twisting his lips. War cries and the roar of guns hammered at his ears. The lanky Texan fired as fast as he could lever cartridges into the chamber. He squinted into the smoke filling the junipers like a winter fog.

At the last moment, the Comanche war party broke under the murderous fire and swerved to the right in a broad circle. Even as they retreated, several Comanche warriors twisted in their saddles and continued firing.

"Whew!" Leeboy said taking a deep breath and looking at Josh.

"You can say that again," Josh replied, hastily reloading the Henry. "And while you're at it, rub that good luck piece for us."

"Reload, men!" Zeke barked, at the same time, capping his Colt. "Kincaid. What about Crocker?"

Seconds later, Kincaid shouted back, "Dead, Lieutenant!"

Zeke grimaced. That left five rifles, counting the woman.

"What about you, Gian-nah-tah?"

"Not hurt."

Beyond range of the repeating rifles, the Comanche milled about, building their courage for another attack.

Keeping his eyes on the Indians, Zeke said, "What do you think?"

Josh studied the Comanches wildly brandishing their rifles over their heads. "Reckon they'll be back."

"We got six that time. Odds are better now," Leeboy put in. "Why, I figure—"

The crack of a Henry and a strangled cry from behind cut him off. Both Josh and Leeboy stiffened and looked back.

"Stay here," Zeke snapped, racing back through the juniper.

Moments later, his voice rang out. "She's fine. Knocked herself a Comanche from the rim."

Josh glanced at Leeboy with a grin. Suddenly, the yelp of a war cry jerked him back around. "Better hurry yourself up, Zeke, unless you want us to do your job for you. They're coming back!" he shouted, tugging the butt of the rifle snugly into his shoulder and squinting along the barrel, setting the sight on the warrior in the middle of the charge. He flexed his fingers about the pistol grip. "I got the one in middle."

"I'll take the one to his left," Leeboy announced.

Kincaid called out. "That gives me the one on the outside.

Zeke pushed through the juniper and took his place. He chuckled. "Reckon I'll try for the one on the other side."

The determined warriors began firing when they hit the water fifty yards distant. Puffs of smoke from the black powder ballooned around the muzzles of the rifles. Josh could hear the slugs slicing through the junipers, thudding into trunks, tearing off branches.

Josh called out. "Fire when they leave the water and don't stop firing."

The charging horses sent sprays of water in every direction, those in the lead almost obscuring those behind. Josh ran his tongue over his dry lips and tightened his finger on the trigger. He steadied the blade sight on the Comanche's chest and waited, one eye on his target, the other at the rapidly shrinking distance between the warriors and the water's edge.

The moment the lead warrior's horse touched the shore, one Colt cracked and four rifles boomed, and four warriors were slammed out of their saddles.

Sweat ran down Josh's face, stinging his eyes, but he kept firing. Every second, he expected the charge to fall apart, but the screaming warriors drove their war ponies mercilessly, holding tight with their legs and firing their rifles.

Six made it to the claystone and charged into the junipers.

Josh rolled aside, barely dodging a pony's hooves. Muttering a curse, he snapped off a shot, catching the Comanche brave in the back of his head.

At the same time, one of the braves leaped from the back of his horse and slammed Leeboy to the ground. Leeboy quickly rolled to his feet and using his Henry like a club, crushed the Comanche's head as the brave struggled to his feet.

Shots rang out from Emmeline's post. Josh charged into the juniper and hackberry, shouldering the wiry limbs aside. He skidded to a halt when he burst out of the thick growth. One warrior lay on the ground, and another was advancing on foot toward Emmeline who was frantically levering cartridges into the chamber and pulling the trigger, but the rifle continued to misfire.

"Emmeline!" Josh shouted, throwing his rifle to his shoulder and drawing down on the Comanche brave. He pulled the trigger. The firing pin fell on an empty chamber with a chilling click.

The surprise on the Comanche's face turned into a sneer when he realized what had happened. He jerked his rifle to his shoulder and swung it around on Josh.

Before he could pull the trigger, a rifle cracked from the juniper to the left, sending the warrior sprawling to the red claystone, dead before he hit the ground.

Josh and Emmeline looked around as Luis Alvarado Elizio Guadalupe Martinez stepped from behind the wall of juniper, a smoking rifle in his hands and a broad grin on his face.

Chapter Twenty

A deathly silence lay over the box canyon. Gunsmoke drifted lazily upward into the clear sky.

Zeke, his Colt holstered, approached. "You two all right?"

Josh looked at Emmeline who forced a weak smile and nodded. "Reckon so. Anyone hurt up there?"

"The sergeant. Dead," Leeboy replied, stepping into the clearing. "But he got his man."

"Kincaid?" Zeke asked.

"If he was the sergeant."

Shaking his head slowly, Zeke said, "He was a good man. A good soldier."

Josh and Leeboy frowned at each other. Incredulous, Josh said, "You were going to kill him yourself. You said so."

Zeke looked at him in dismay. "Don't you understand? That was different. I respected him as a good soldier, a fine sergeant. It's just I didn't plan to share the gold with him."

Josh was speechless.

Leeboy snorted and glared at Zeke. "I don't reckon I could see it back then, Zeke, but you was worthless as a boy and just as worthless now. Ain't you got no feelings for anyone except yourself?"

Zeke's eyes narrowed. "One man's opinion."

"Nope. Two," Josh drawled. "What about the gold now? Looks to me like we got ourselves a Mexican standoff."

For several moments, Zeke studied his two old friends. Finally a faint smile ticked up the edges of his lips. "I suppose we do."

"And," Josh added, his words filled with defiance, "we're taking the gold back with us. To help the invasion of Galveston."

Zeke stiffened slightly, then relaxed. A soft chuckle rolled from his lips. "Sometimes you throw a steer, sometimes it throws you. I know when I'm licked."

Nodding, Josh turned to Emmeline. "Are you—"

Leeboy shouted, "Josh!"

Shucking his Colt and spinning into a crouch, he heard Zeke's sixgun roar. He fired twice at Zeke and then spun back around when a rifle roared from behind.

But there was no one standing. Gian-nah-tah lay sprawled on the ground, a bloody hole in his forehead.

He jerked back around, hammer cocked, ready to fire. Zeke lay on the ground. An anguished grimace contorted Josh's face when he realized what had happened.

"Leeboy!" Emmeline screamed and rushed past Josh to the red-headed cowpoke lying on his back, clutching his stomach.

Josh looked back at Zeke, then dropped to one knee beside his partner. His heart thudded in his chest and fear for Leeboy clogged his throat. "Leeboy. Can you hear me?"

Leeboy opened his eyes slowly. He parted his lips. His words were a whisper. "Don't reckon that lucky gold piece did me much good this time, huh, partner?" He looked up into the blue sky and tried to laugh. "Wouldn't you know?"

Josh and Emmeline looked up. Overhead, six black crows flew northward.

Leeboy coughed. His words slurred, he muttered, "Remember, Josh. Six crows. I–I told you—that wasn't no old wife's tale." His eyes fluttered shut, and then he died.

Emmeline frowned up at Josh. "Six crows? What did he mean by that?"

Woodenly, Josh muttered, "A foolish superstition. One's bad, two's luck, three's health, four's wealth, five's sickness, and six is death." He blinked back the tears. "Just a silly superstition."

Emmeline broke into sobs as Josh hurried to Zeke. He holstered his sixgun and knelt by his old friend, eyeing the two bloody holes in his friend's chest with remorse. "Zeke—I—I didn't know. I thought you were pulling down on me. I—"

Zeke tried to laugh, but all he could do was spit up blood. "Not your fault, Josh. Not—a bit. I'da figured the same thing. I just couldn't let that heathen Apache shoot the kid who used to run barefoot through the woods with me." His eyelids flickered. He dragged his tongue over his lips. "Too bad you—wouldn't take my offer. Saved us all a heap of pain."

Josh laid his hand on Zeke's arm. "Anything I can do for you?"

Painfully, turning his head so he could see Leeboy, he whispered, "He hurt bad?"

Eyes burning, Josh swallowed the lump in his throat. "Dead. Looks like when you got the Apache, his shot went wild and hit Leeboy in the belly."

Zeke squeezed his eyes shut, then opened them to look up at Josh. He spoke, but he had to force each word from his lips. Hesitantly, he replied, "Didn't mean for that to happen." He blinked at the tears filling his eyes. "Truth is, I couldn't have shot either of you no-goods."

"I know," Josh whispered. "I know."

"But, you can do one more thing for me."

Tears blurred Josh's vision. He managed to choke out a word. "What?"

"Bury me next to Leeboy. That way, neither one of

us will get lonesome on that road to wherever we're going."

Josh tried to speak, but the words couldn't get past the burning knot in his throat. Before he could reply, Zeke died.

Behind Josh, Emmeline continued to sob over Leeboy.

By sunset, their task was complete. Josh, with Emmeline on one side and Luis on the other, stood at the head of Leeboy's and Zeke's graves. To the west, nature had cast a spectacular array of pinks and oranges and lavenders across the heavens in broad, bold strokes.

"When we was boys," he whispered, more to himself than the others, "we used to sit on the banks of the old Colorado River and watch sunsets just like this. And then one of us would jump to his feet and take off running. And he'd let out with a shout, 'Last one back to the barn's a rotten egg.' "

Emmeline laid her hand on his arm. "What will you do now?"

"Take the gold back, I reckon. And then, who knows?" He looked at her. "What about you? Your pa's team should be at Fort Chadbourne."

She stared at the graves and whispered, "I wouldn't know what to do then. Pa bought a little ranch near Mason. I don't know if I'd have the heart to run it." She looked up at Josh hopefully.

"I will help," Luis put in. "I have no place to go."

Josh glanced down at the Mexican. He remembered what Leeboy always said, "Everybody needs someone." And then, Josh knew exactly what he was going to do. Suddenly energized, he said, "Tell you what. Let's get this gold back in the cave for tonight, and tomorrow we'll head back." He smiled at Emmeline. "I figure that three folks like us with nobody waiting should stick together. That way, we'll always have each other. Don't you think so? Together, we can build a nice little ranch."

Emmeline beamed. She squeezed his arm. "Yes, I most certainly do. Together," she added.

Josh grinned down at Luis. "And what about you, youngster? You want to go along with the two of us?"

The broad smile that exploded across Luis Alvarado Elizio Guadalupe Martinez's face was answer enough.